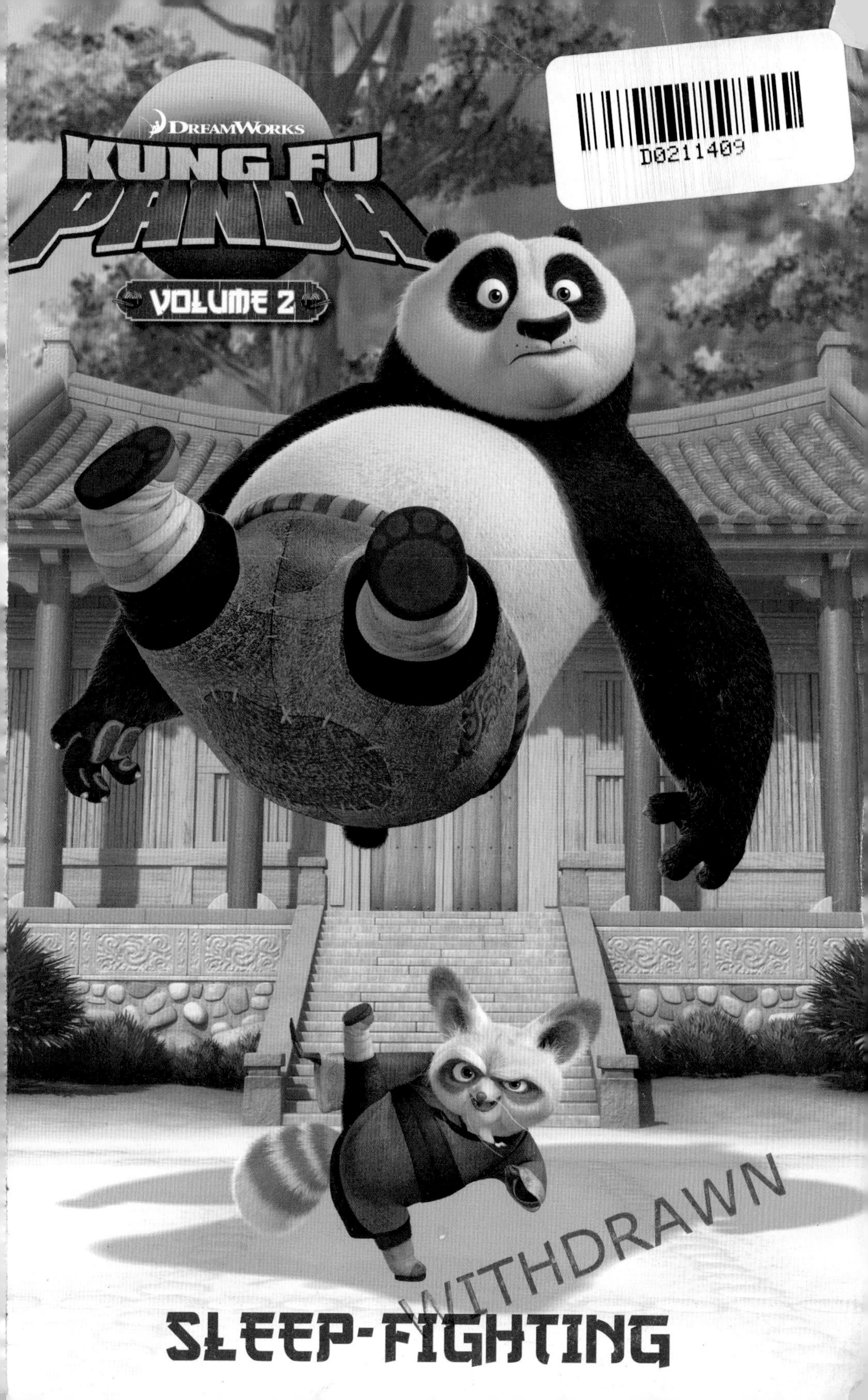
DreamWorks
KUNG FU PANDA
VOLUME 2
D0211409
WITHDRAWN
SLEEP-FIGHTING

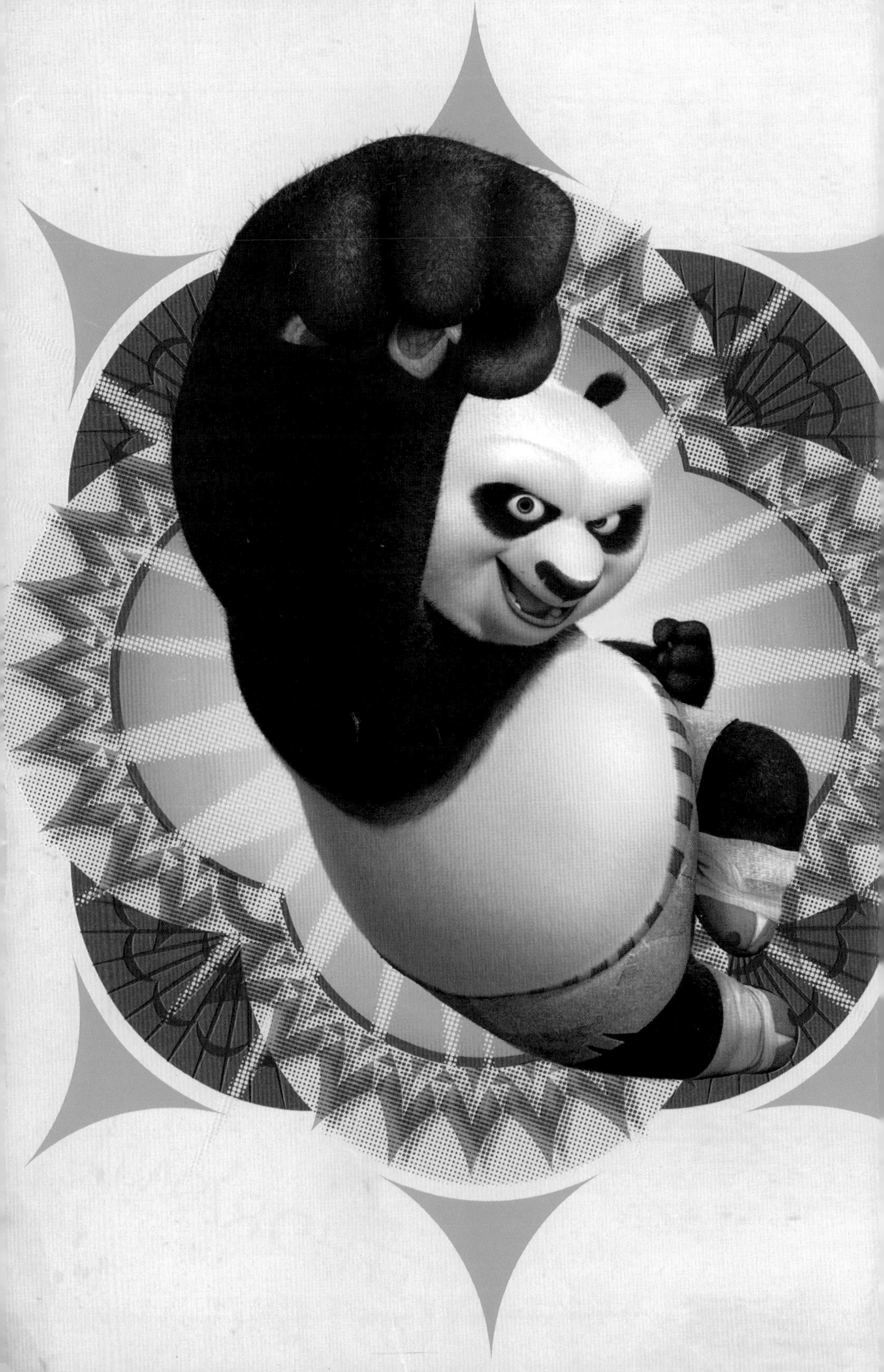

# DREAMWORKS KUNG FU PANDA

## VOLUME 2

# SLEEP-FIGHTING

## 'WAKE ME UP BEFORE YOU PO PO'

**SCRIPT** Simon Furman
**ART** Lee Robinson
**LETTERING** Jim Campbell

## PLUS BONUS STORY:
## 'NO REST FOR THE WICKED'

By Simon Furman
and Philip Murphy

WELCOME TO THE VALLEY OF PEACE! IF YOU HAVE ANY TROUBLE, YOU MIGHT WANT TO ASK THESE GUYS FOR A BIT OF KUNG FU HELP!

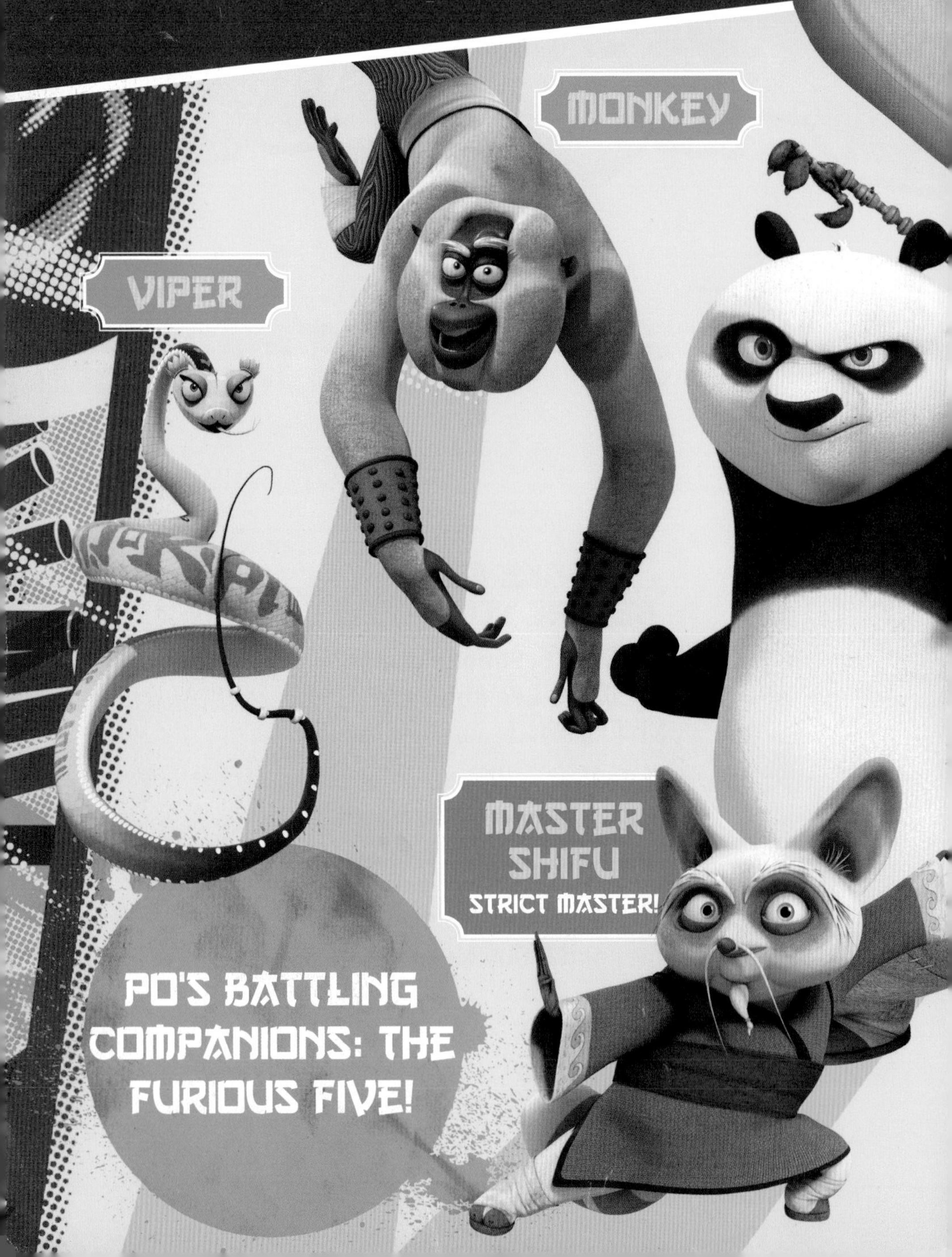
MONKEY
VIPER
MASTER SHIFU
STRICT MASTER!
PO'S BATTLING COMPANIONS: THE FURIOUS FIVE!

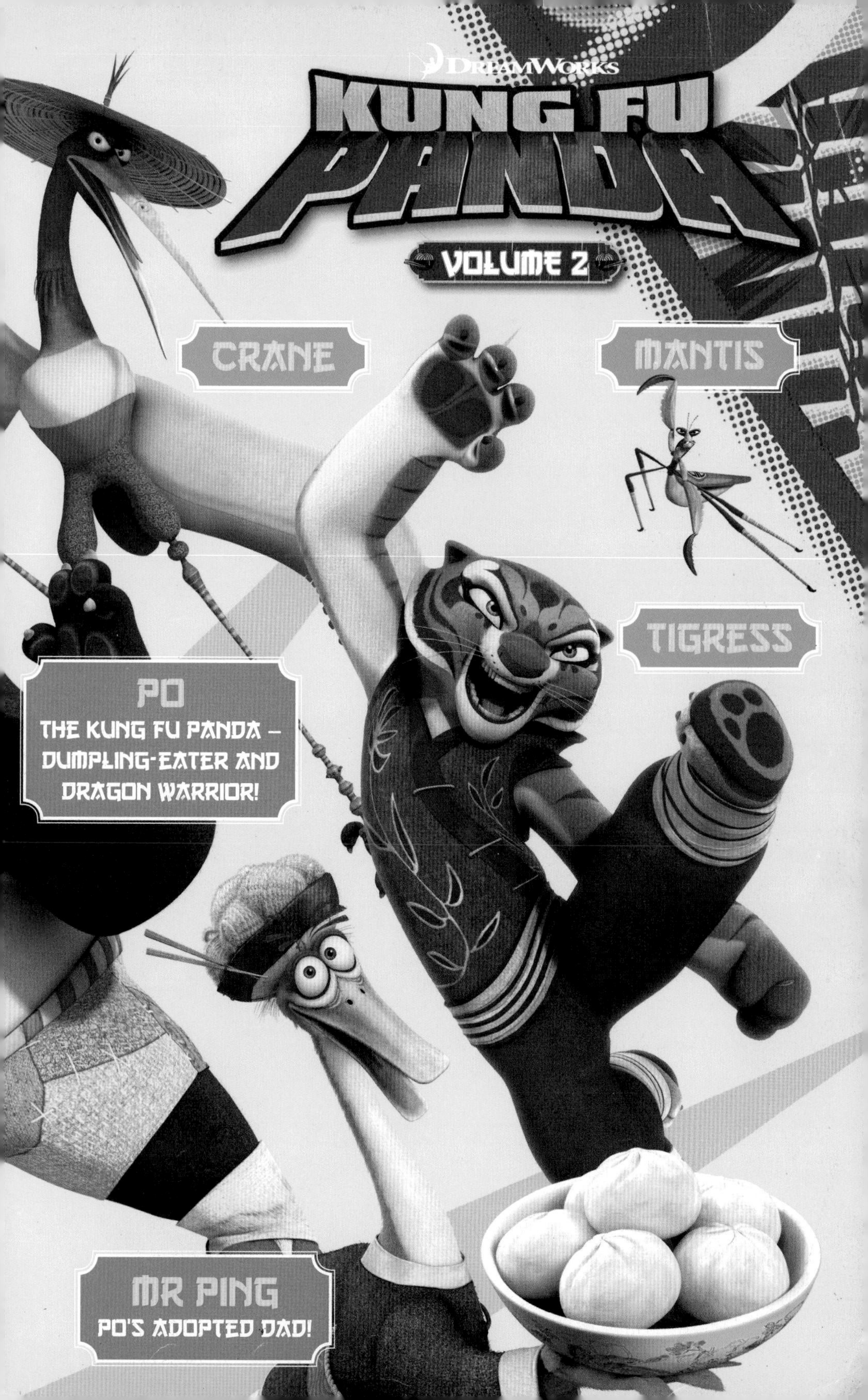
DreamWorks
KUNG FU PANDA
VOLUME 2
CRANE
MANTIS
TIGRESS
PO
THE KUNG FU PANDA –
DUMPLING-EATER AND
DRAGON WARRIOR!
MR PING
PO'S ADOPTED DAD!

TITAN COMICS

SENIOR EDITOR
Martin Eden

PRODUCTION MANAGER
Obi Onuora

PRODUCTION SUPERVISORS
Maria James
Jackie Flook

PRODUCTION ASSISTANT
Peter James

STUDIO MANAGER
Selina Juneja

SENIOR SALES MANAGER
Steve Tothill

MARKETING MANAGER
Ricky Claydon

PUBLISHING MANAGER
Darryl Tothill

PUBLISHING DIRECTOR
Chris Teather

OPERATIONS DIRECTOR
Leigh Baulch

EXECUTIVE DIRECTOR
Vivian Cheung

PUBLISHER
Nick Landau

ISBN: 9781782762690
Published by Titan Comics,
a division of Titan Publishing Group Ltd.
144 Southwark St. London, SE1 0UP

10 9 8 7 6 5 4 3 2 1

First printed in China in December 2015.

A CIP catalogue record for this title is available from the British Library.

Titan Comics. TC0575

Special thanks to Corinne Combs, Barbara Layman, Lawrence Hamashima, and all at DreamWorks, also Donna Askem.

# WAKE ME UP BEFORE YOU PO-PO

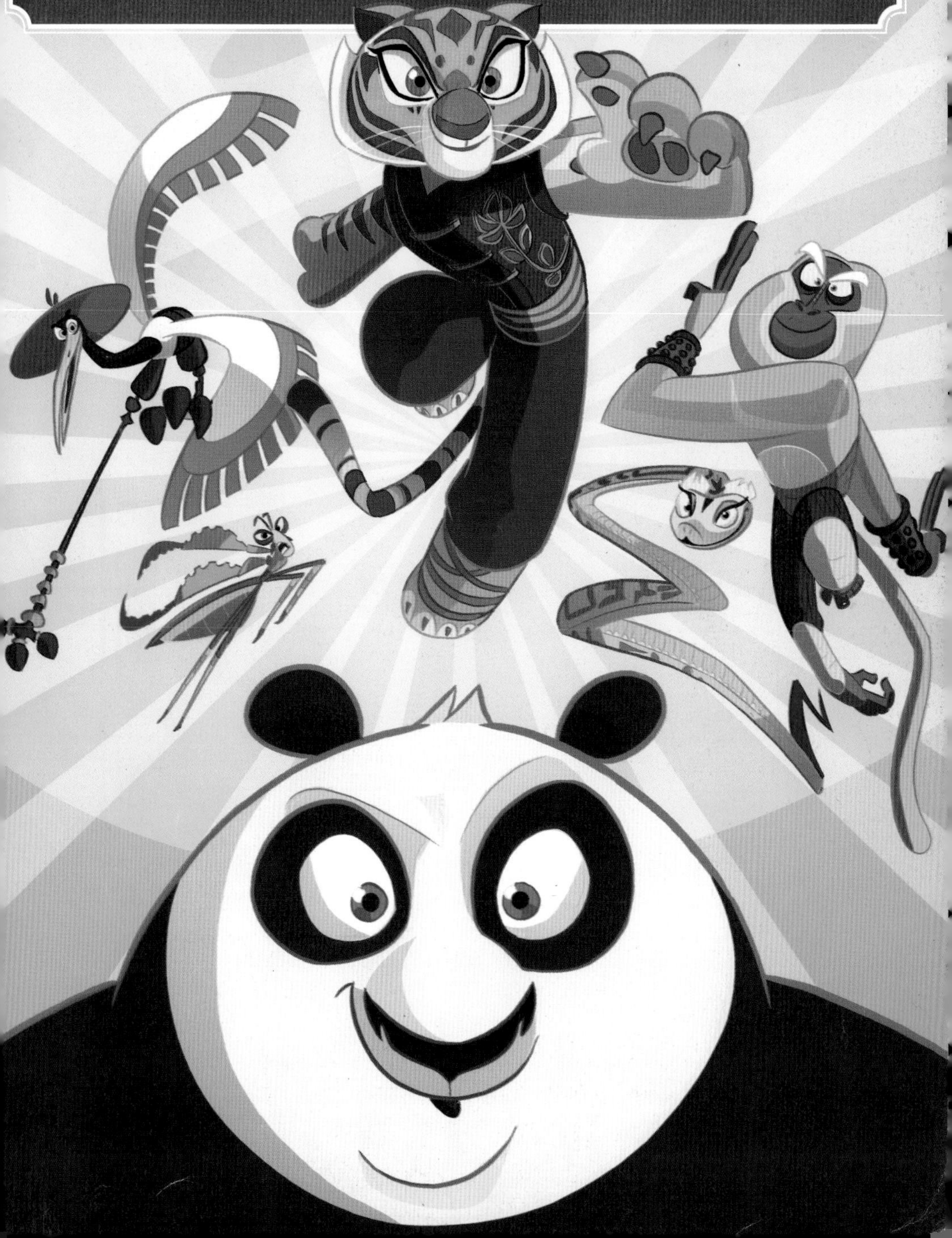

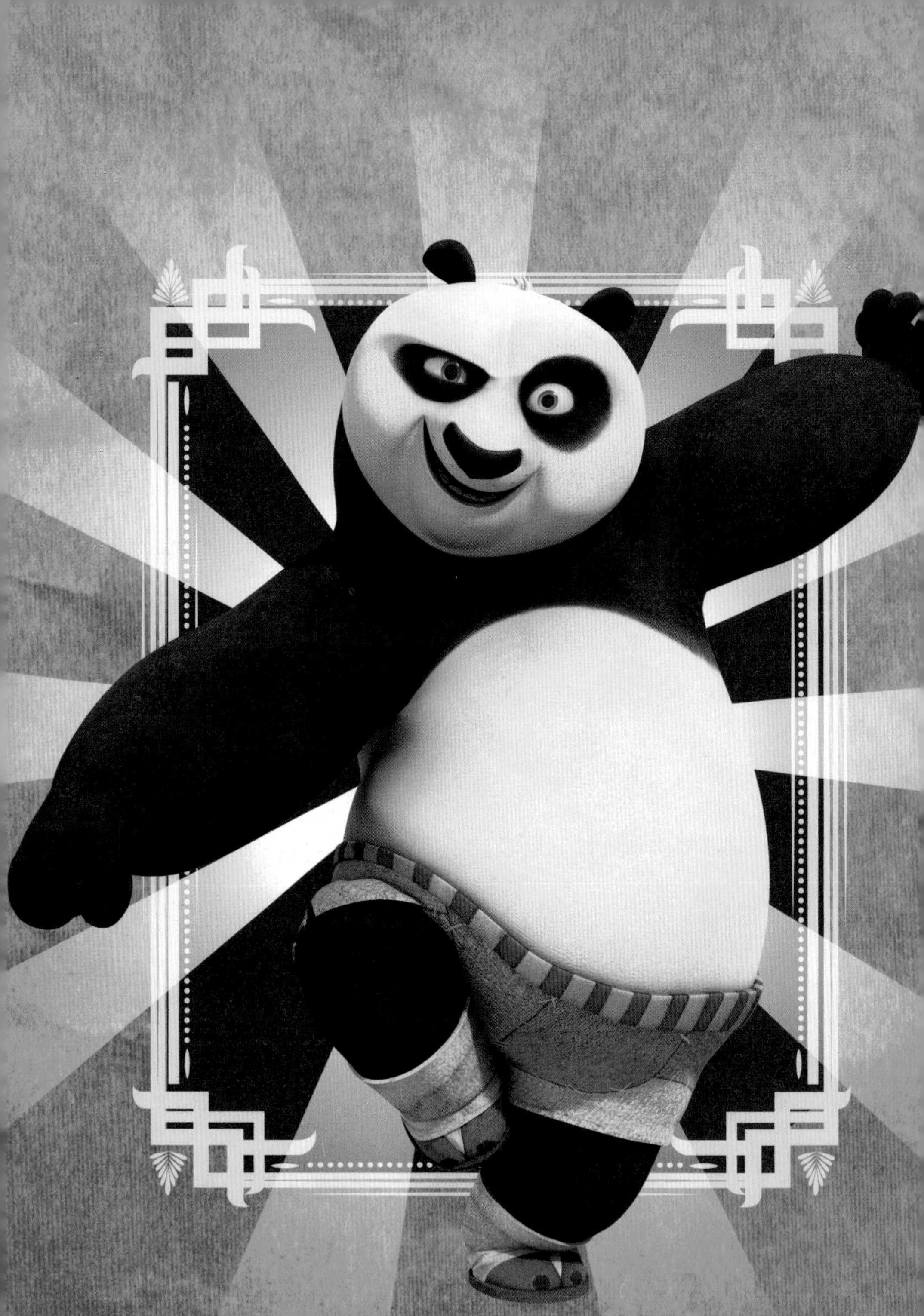

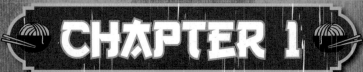

# CHAPTER 1

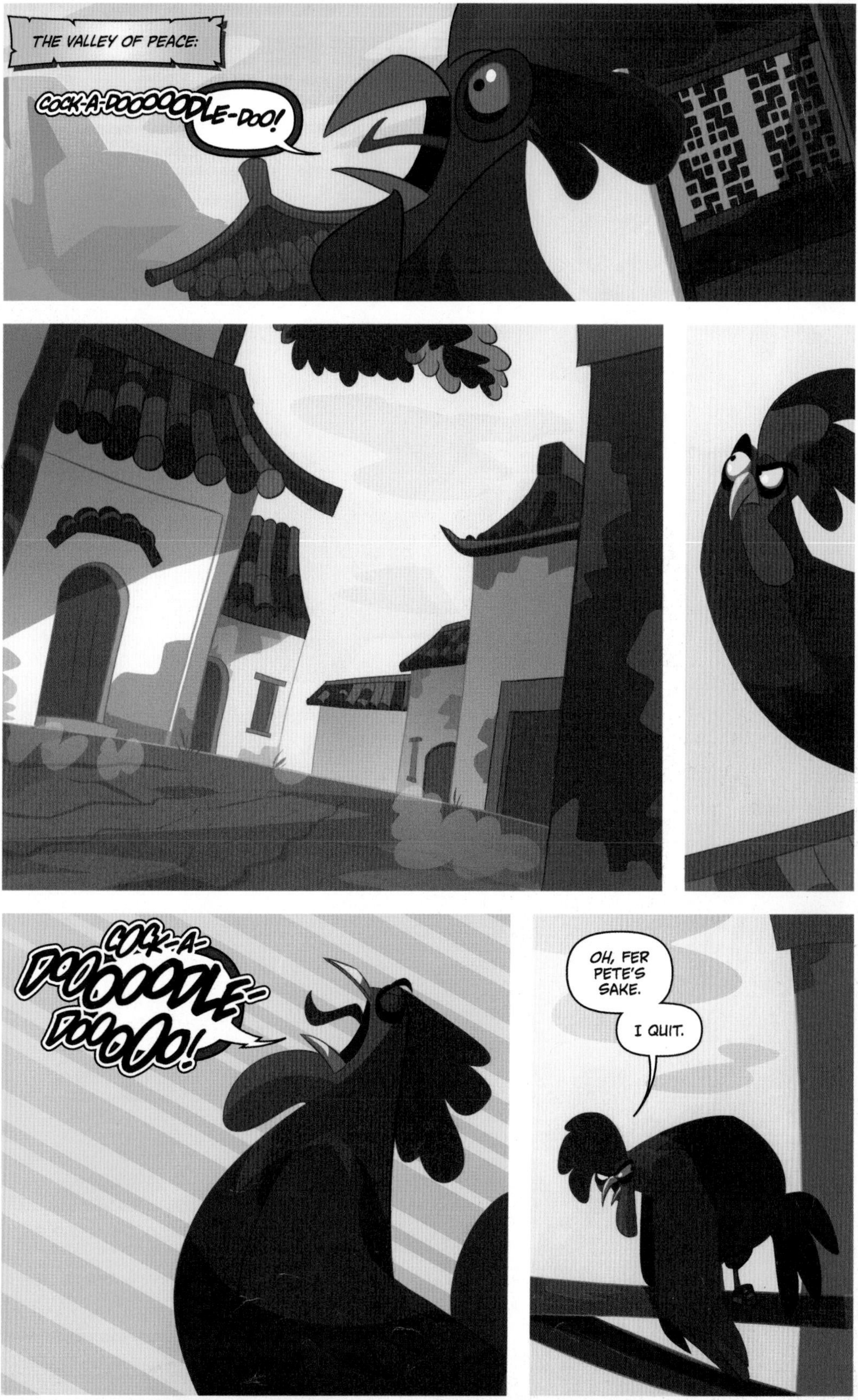
THE VALLEY OF PEACE:
COCK-A-DOOOOOODLE-DOO!
COCK-A-DOOOOODLE-DOOOOO!
OH, FER PETE'S SAKE.
I QUIT.

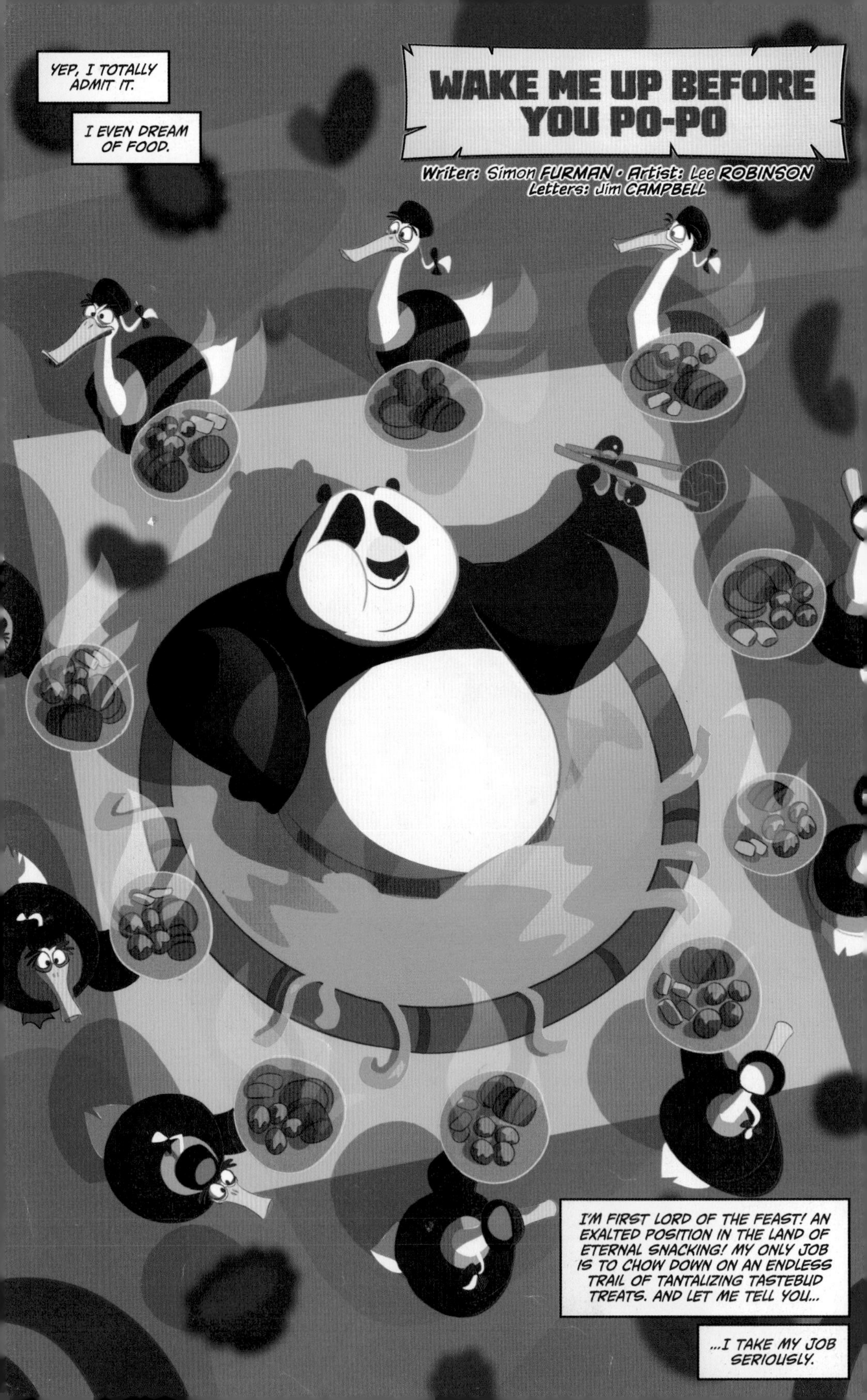

YEP, I TOTALLY ADMIT IT.
I EVEN DREAM OF FOOD.
WAKE ME UP BEFORE YOU PO-PO
Writer: Simon FURMAN • Artist: Lee ROBINSON
Letters: Jim CAMPBELL
I'M FIRST LORD OF THE FEAST! AN EXALTED POSITION IN THE LAND OF ETERNAL SNACKING! MY ONLY JOB IS TO CHOW DOWN ON AN ENDLESS TRAIL OF TANTALIZING TASTEBUD TREATS. AND LET ME TELL YOU...
...I TAKE MY JOB SERIOUSLY.

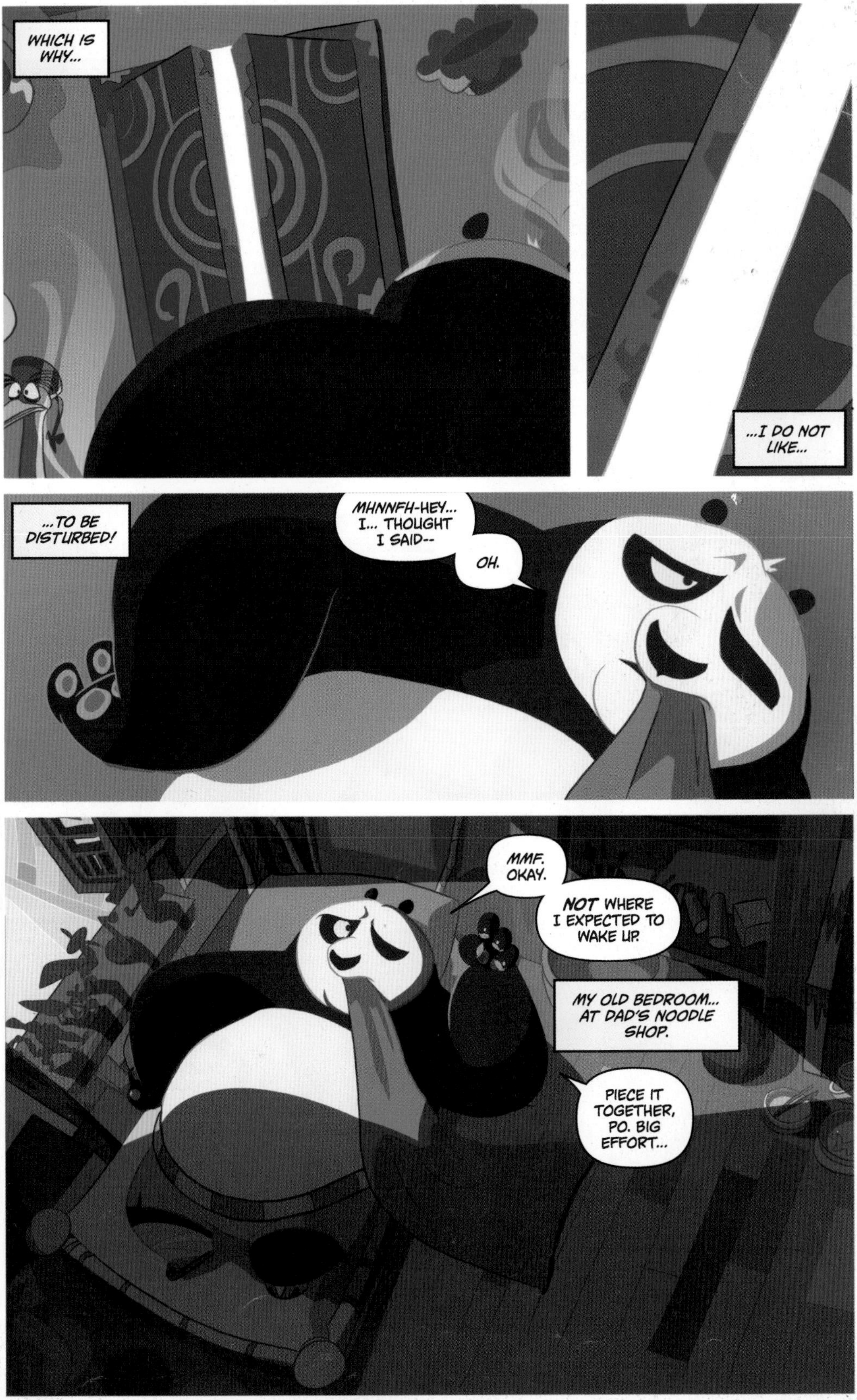
WHICH IS WHY...
...I DO NOT LIKE...
...TO BE DISTURBED!
MHNNFH-HEY... I... THOUGHT I SAID--
OH.
MMF. OKAY.
NOT WHERE I EXPECTED TO WAKE UP.
MY OLD BEDROOM... AT DAD'S NOODLE SHOP.
PIECE IT TOGETHER, PO. BIG EFFORT...

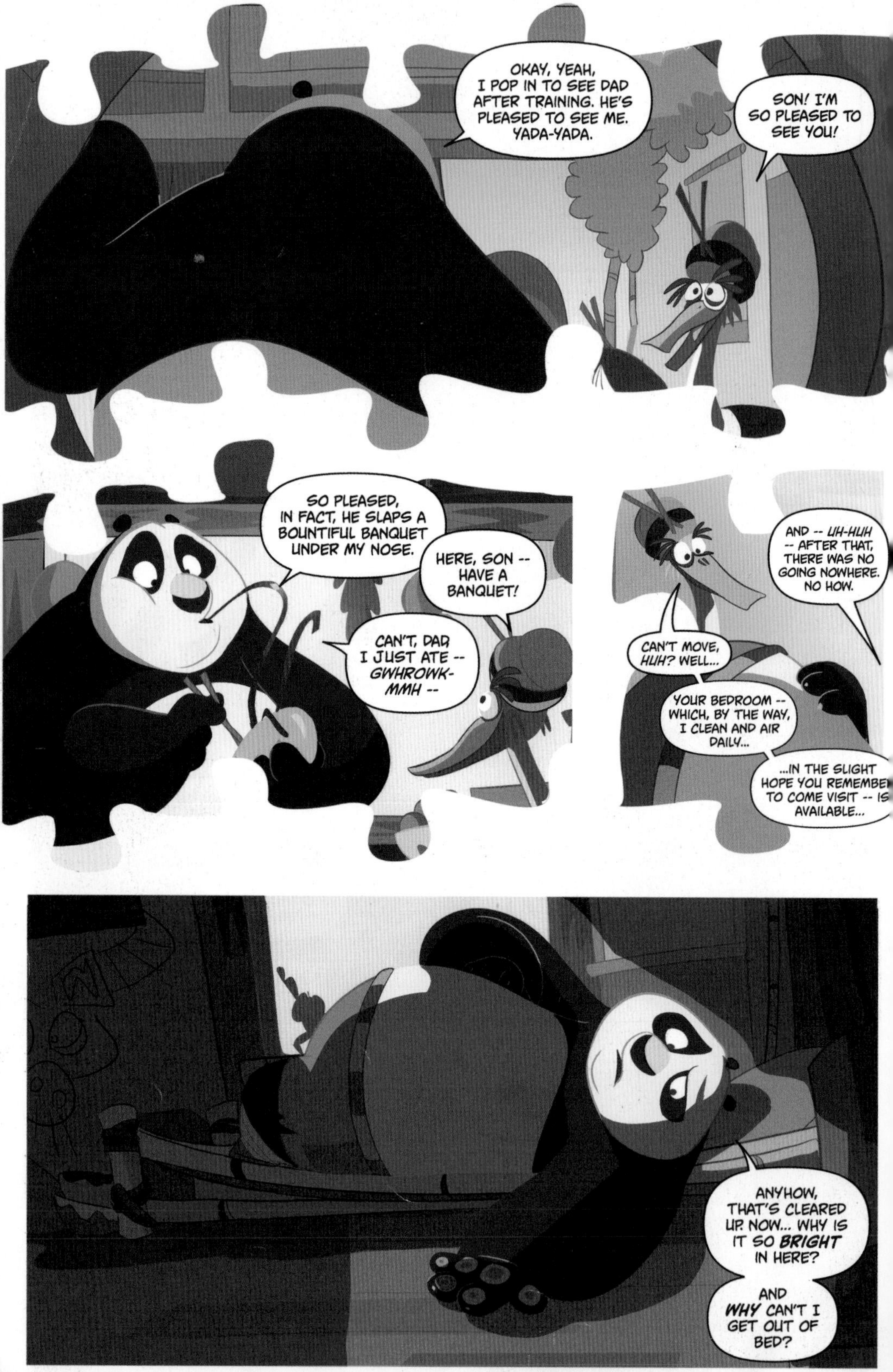
OKAY, YEAH, I POP IN TO SEE DAD AFTER TRAINING. HE'S PLEASED TO SEE ME. YADA-YADA.
SON! I'M SO PLEASED TO SEE YOU!
SO PLEASED, IN FACT, HE SLAPS A BOUNTIFUL BANQUET UNDER MY NOSE.
HERE, SON -- HAVE A BANQUET!
CAN'T, DAD. I JUST ATE -- GWHROWK-MMH --
AND -- UH-HUH -- AFTER THAT, THERE WAS NO GOING NOWHERE. NO HOW.
CAN'T MOVE, HUH? WELL...
YOUR BEDROOM -- WHICH, BY THE WAY, I CLEAN AND AIR DAILY...
...IN THE SLIGHT HOPE YOU REMEMBE TO COME VISIT -- IS AVAILABLE...
ANYHOW, THAT'S CLEARED UP. NOW... WHY IS IT SO BRIGHT IN HERE?
AND WHY CAN'T I GET OUT OF BED?

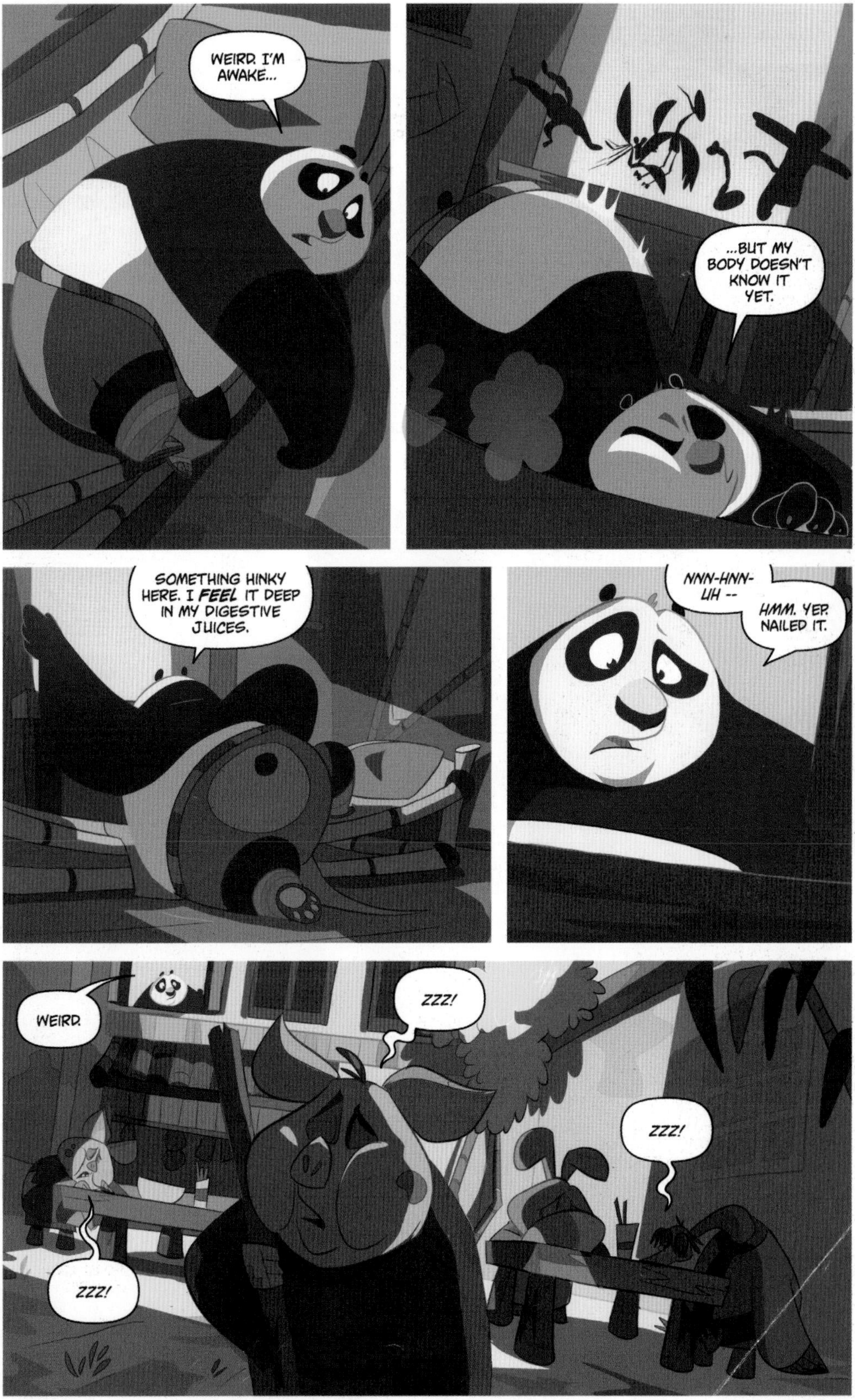
WEIRD. I'M AWAKE...
...BUT MY BODY DOESN'T KNOW IT YET.
SOMETHING HINKY HERE. I *FEEL* IT DEEP IN MY DIGESTIVE JUICES.
*NNN-HNN-UH --*
*HMM.* YEP. NAILED IT.
WEIRD.
*ZZZ!*
*ZZZ!*
*ZZZ!*

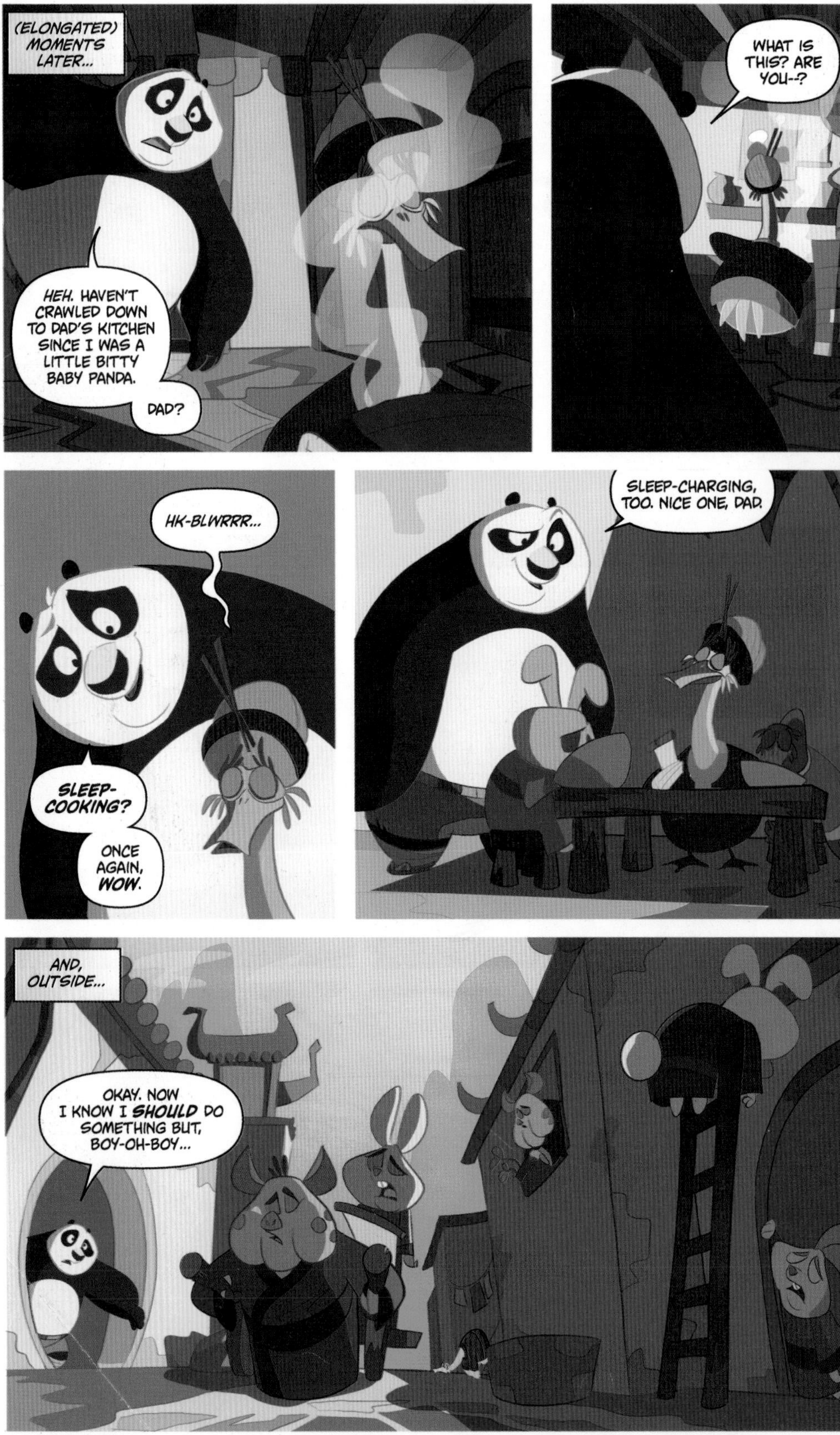
(ELONGATED) MOMENTS LATER...
HEH. HAVEN'T CRAWLED DOWN TO DAD'S KITCHEN SINCE I WAS A LITTLE BITTY BABY PANDA.
DAD?
WHAT IS THIS? ARE YOU--?
HK-BLWRRR...
SLEEP-COOKING?
ONCE AGAIN, WOW.
SLEEP-CHARGING, TOO. NICE ONE, DAD.
AND, OUTSIDE...
OKAY. NOW I KNOW I SHOULD DO SOMETHING BUT, BOY-OH-BOY...

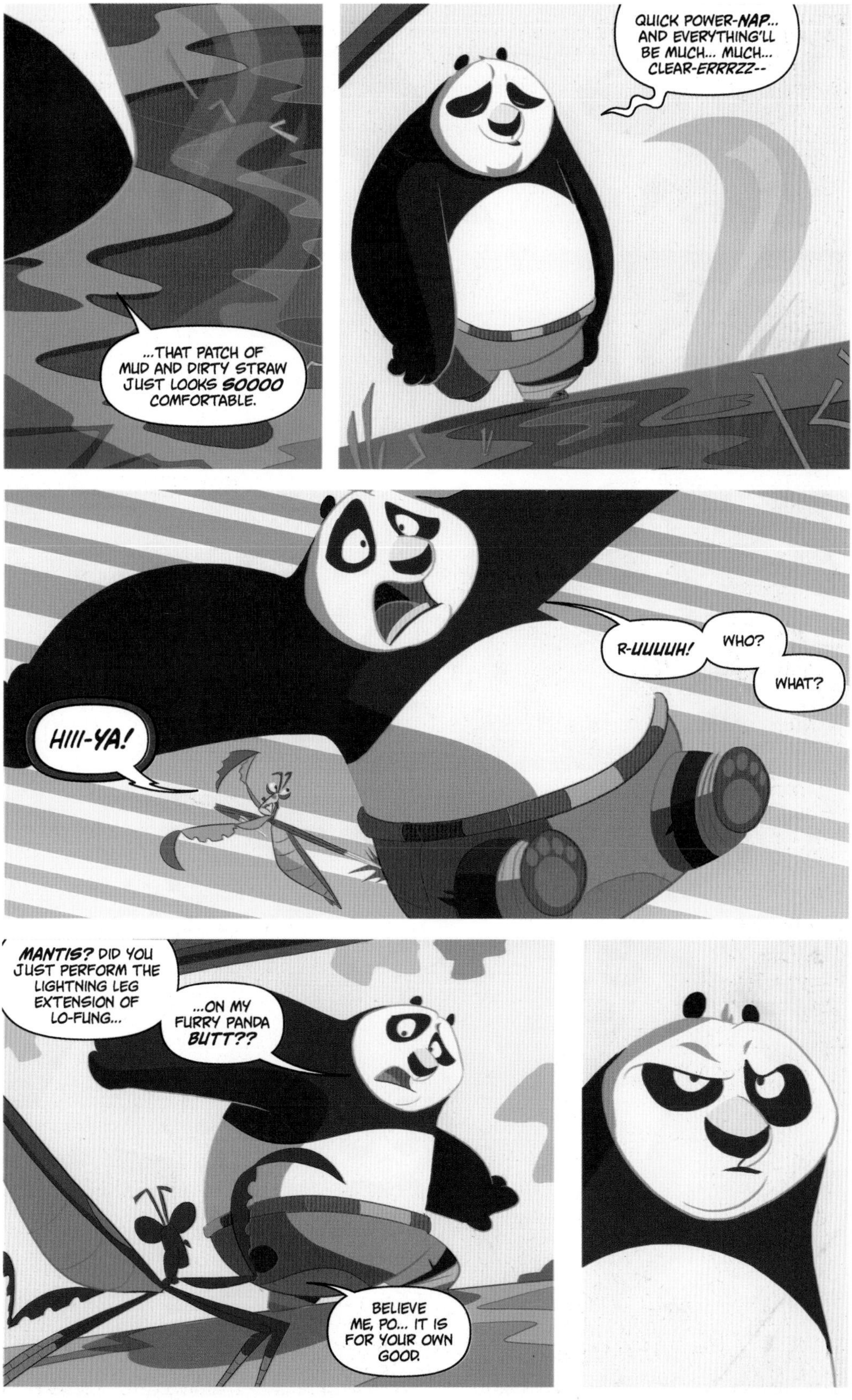
...THAT PATCH OF MUD AND DIRTY STRAW JUST LOOKS SOOOO COMFORTABLE.
QUICK POWER-NAP... AND EVERYTHING'LL BE MUCH... MUCH... CLEAR-ERRRZZ--
HIII-YA!
R-UUUUH!
WHO?
WHAT?
MANTIS? DID YOU JUST PERFORM THE LIGHTNING LEG EXTENSION OF LO-FUNG...
...ON MY FURRY PANDA BUTT??
BELIEVE ME, PO... IT IS FOR YOUR OWN GOOD.

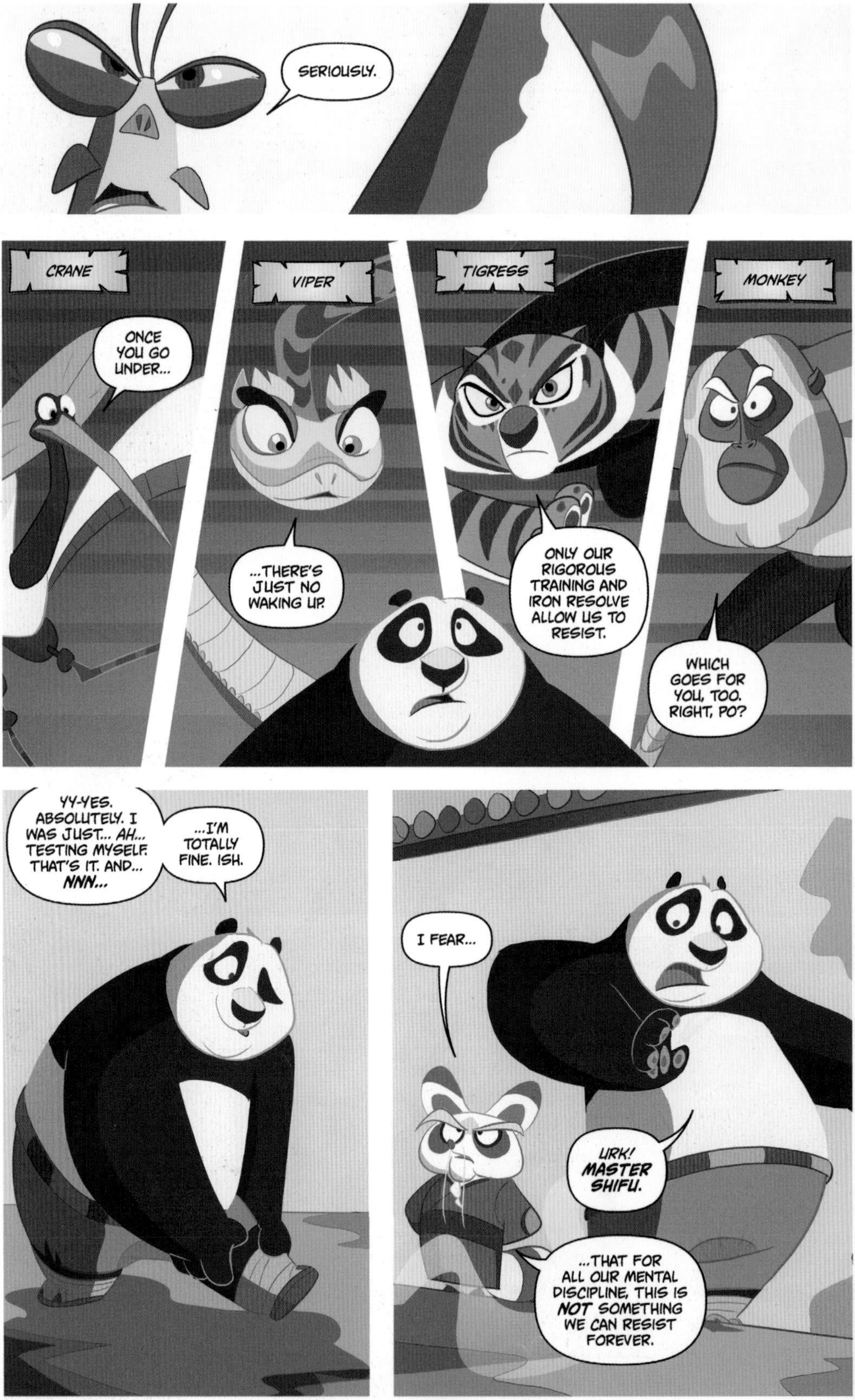
SERIOUSLY.
CRANE
ONCE YOU GO UNDER...
VIPER
...THERE'S JUST NO WAKING UP.
TIGRESS
ONLY OUR RIGOROUS TRAINING AND IRON RESOLVE ALLOW US TO RESIST.
MONKEY
WHICH GOES FOR YOU, TOO. RIGHT, PO?
YY-YES. ABSOLUTELY. I WAS JUST... AH... TESTING MYSELF. THAT'S IT. AND... NNN...
...I'M TOTALLY FINE. ISH.
I FEAR...
URK! MASTER SHIFU.
...THAT FOR ALL OUR MENTAL DISCIPLINE, THIS IS NOT SOMETHING WE CAN RESIST FOREVER.

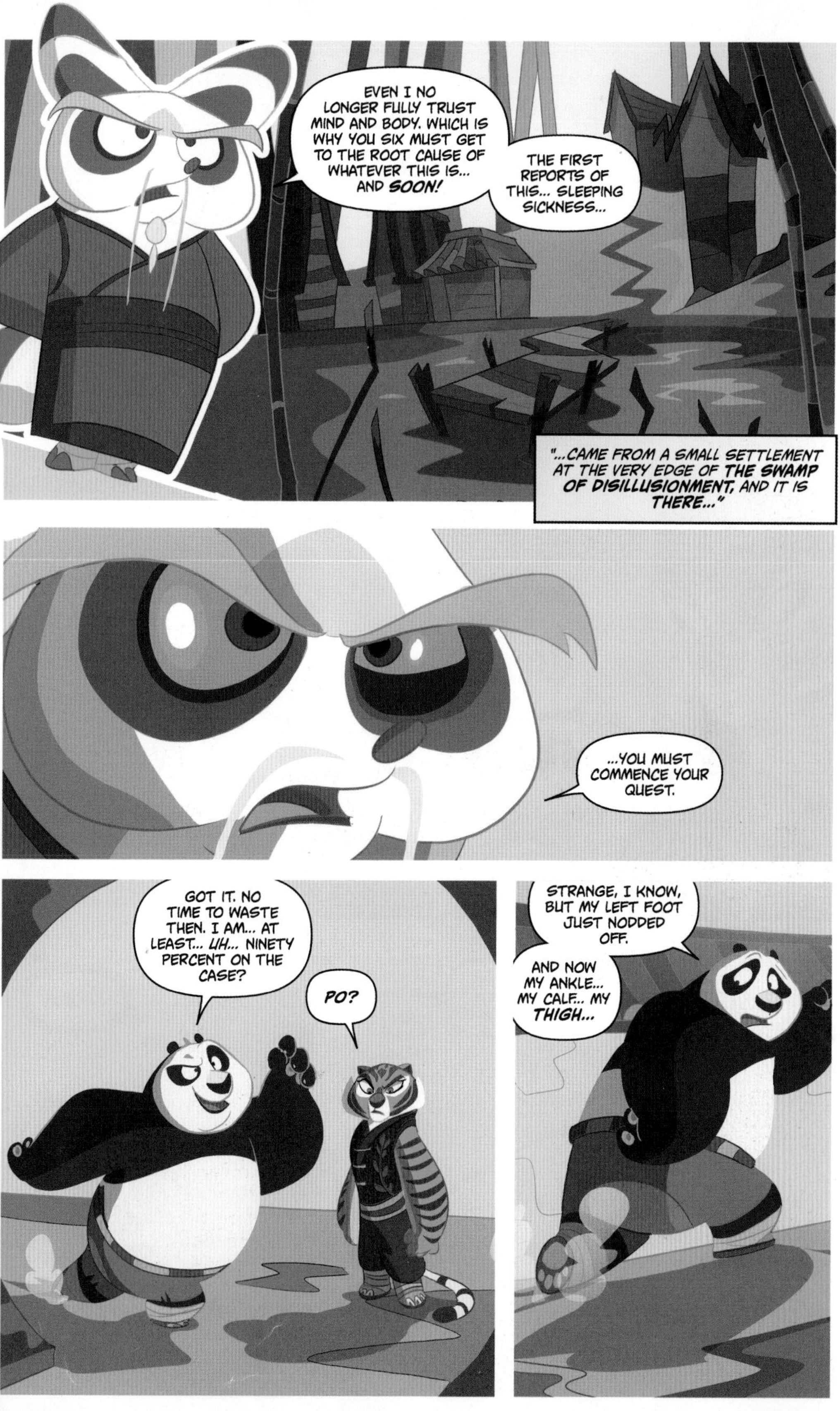
EVEN I NO LONGER FULLY TRUST MIND AND BODY. WHICH IS WHY YOU SIX MUST GET TO THE ROOT CAUSE OF WHATEVER THIS IS... AND SOON!
THE FIRST REPORTS OF THIS... SLEEPING SICKNESS...
"...CAME FROM A SMALL SETTLEMENT AT THE VERY EDGE OF THE SWAMP OF DISILLUSIONMENT, AND IT IS THERE..."
...YOU MUST COMMENCE YOUR QUEST.
GOT IT. NO TIME TO WASTE THEN. I AM... AT LEAST... UH... NINETY PERCENT ON THE CASE?
PO?
STRANGE, I KNOW, BUT MY LEFT FOOT JUST NODDED OFF.
AND NOW MY ANKLE... MY CALF... MY THIGH...

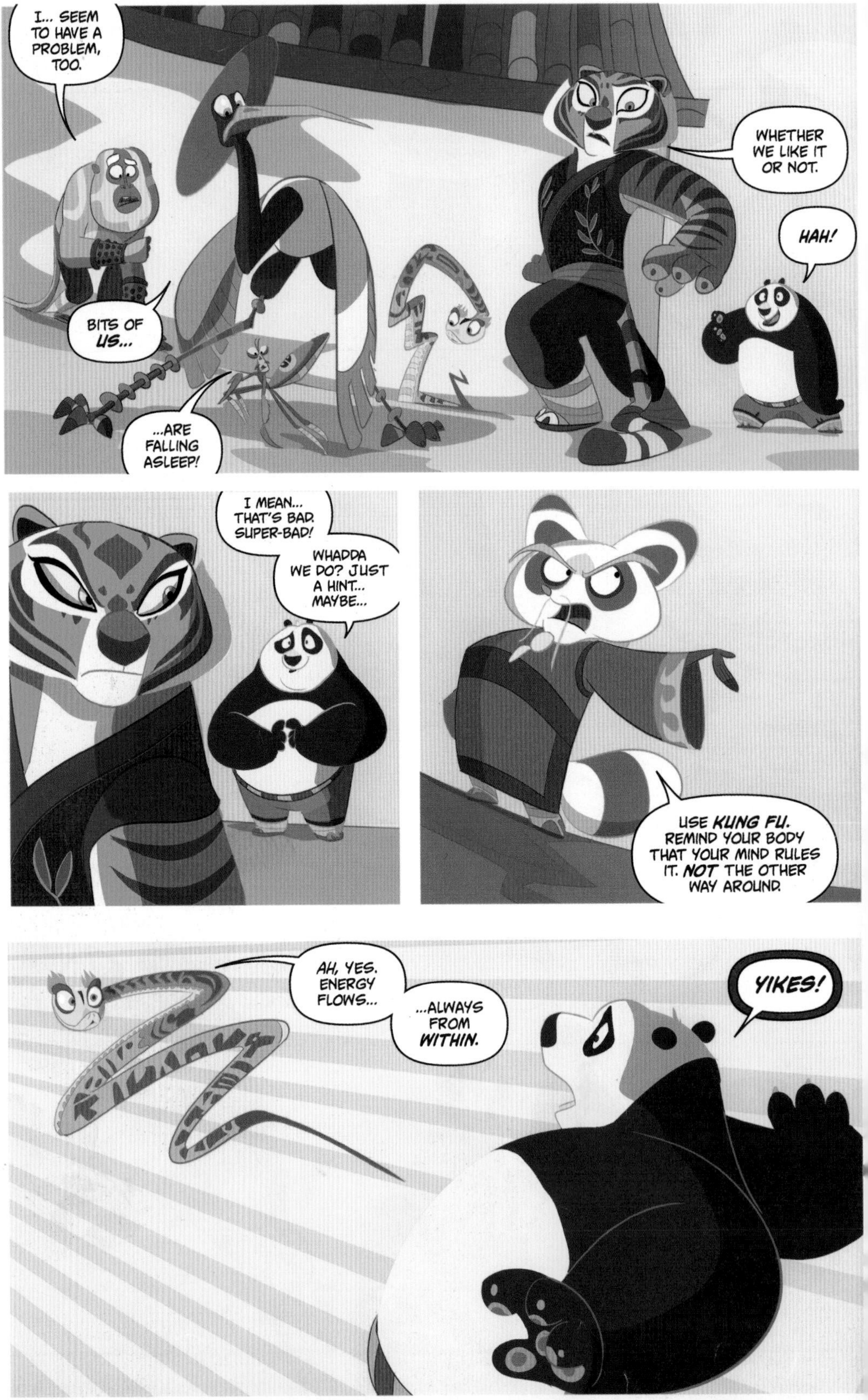
I... SEEM TO HAVE A PROBLEM, TOO.
BITS OF US...
...ARE FALLING ASLEEP!
WHETHER WE LIKE IT OR NOT.
HAH!
I MEAN... THAT'S BAD. SUPER-BAD!
WHADDA WE DO? JUST A HINT... MAYBE...
USE KUNG FU. REMIND YOUR BODY THAT YOUR MIND RULES IT. NOT THE OTHER WAY AROUND.
AH, YES. ENERGY FLOWS...
...ALWAYS FROM WITHIN.
YIKES!

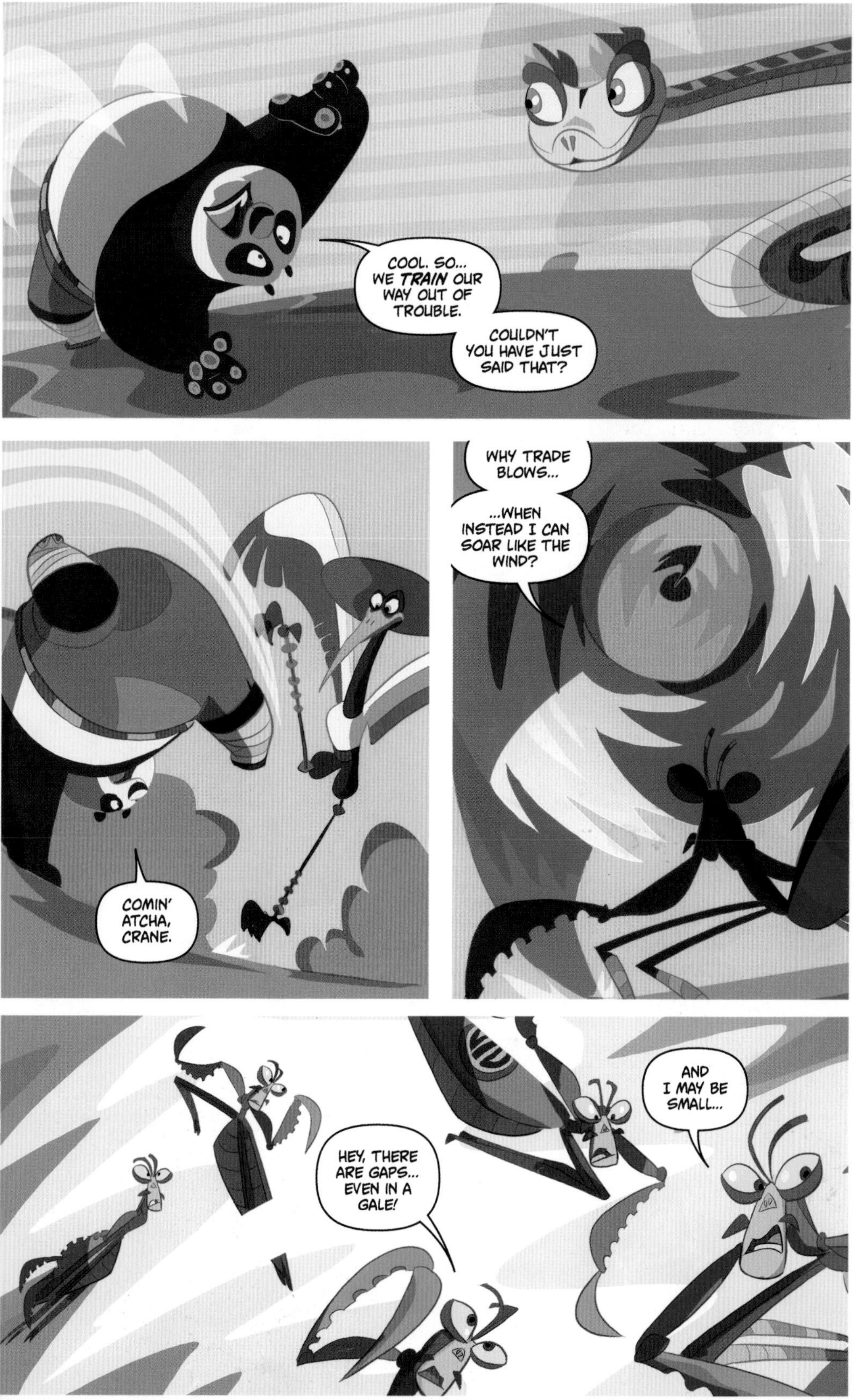
COOL. SO... WE TRAIN OUR WAY OUT OF TROUBLE.
COULDN'T YOU HAVE JUST SAID THAT?
COMIN' ATCHA, CRANE.
WHY TRADE BLOWS...
...WHEN INSTEAD I CAN SOAR LIKE THE WIND?
HEY, THERE ARE GAPS... EVEN IN A GALE!
AND I MAY BE SMALL...

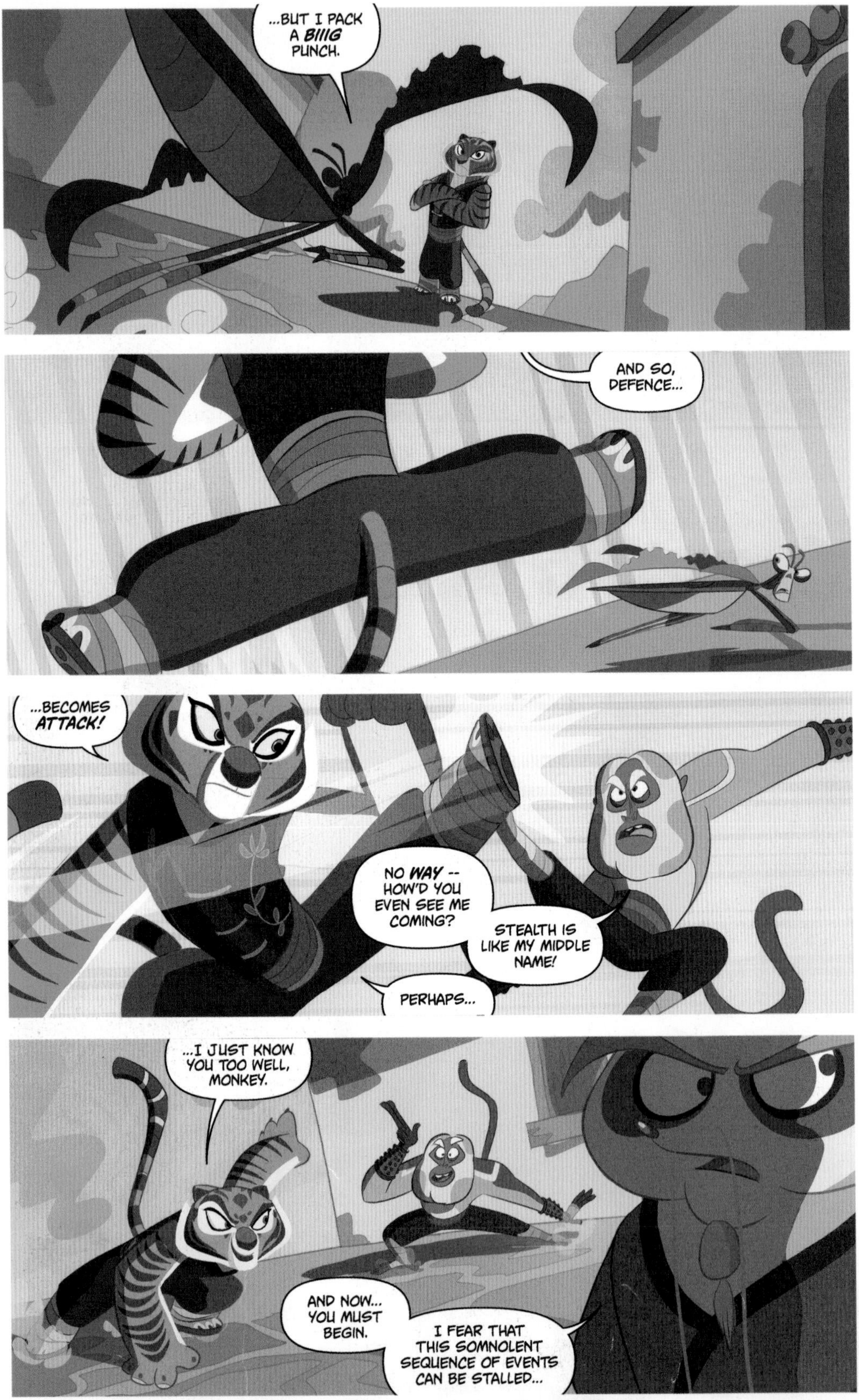

...BUT I PACK A BIIIG PUNCH.
AND SO, DEFENCE...
...BECOMES ATTACK!
NO WAY -- HOW'D YOU EVEN SEE ME COMING?
STEALTH IS LIKE MY MIDDLE NAME!
PERHAPS...
...I JUST KNOW YOU TOO WELL, MONKEY.
AND NOW... YOU MUST BEGIN.
I FEAR THAT THIS SOMNOLENT SEQUENCE OF EVENTS CAN BE STALLED...

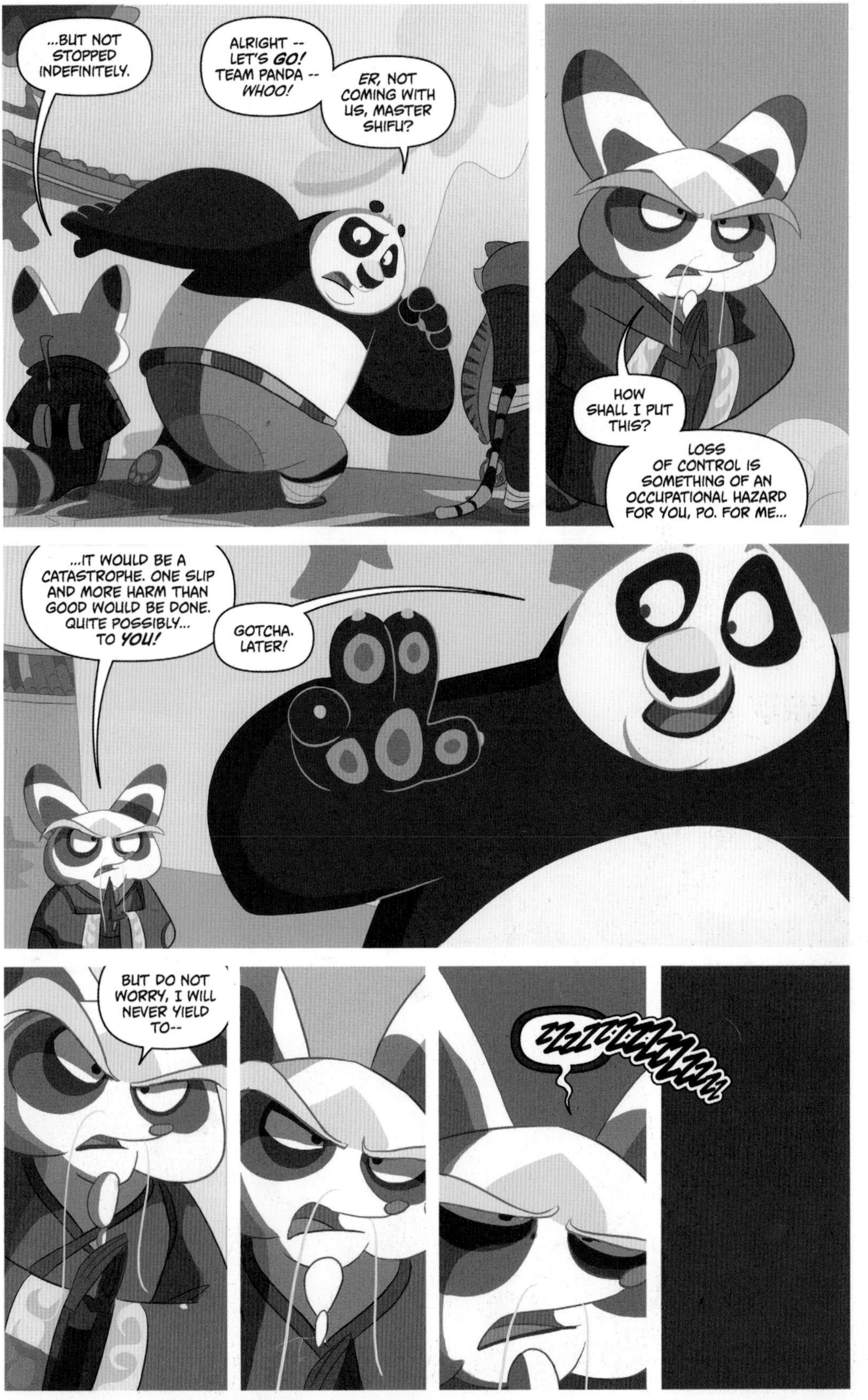

...BUT NOT STOPPED INDEFINITELY.
ALRIGHT -- LET'S GO! TEAM PANDA -- WHOO!
ER, NOT COMING WITH US, MASTER SHIFU?
HOW SHALL I PUT THIS?
LOSS OF CONTROL IS SOMETHING OF AN OCCUPATIONAL HAZARD FOR YOU, PO. FOR ME...
...IT WOULD BE A CATASTROPHE. ONE SLIP AND MORE HARM THAN GOOD WOULD BE DONE. QUITE POSSIBLY... TO YOU!
GOTCHA. LATER!
BUT DO NOT WORRY, I WILL NEVER YIELD TO--
ZZZZZZZZZZZZZZZZZZZ

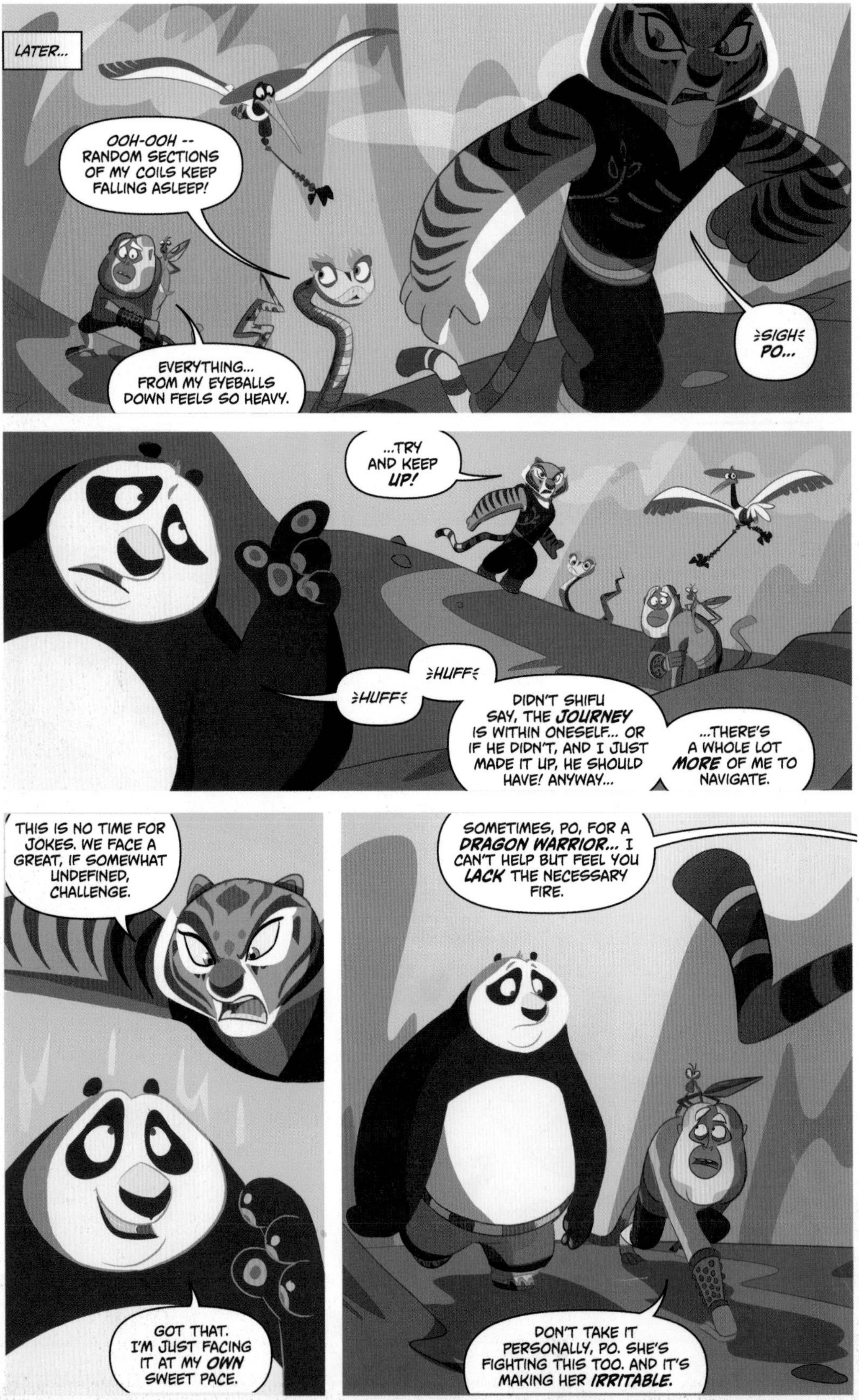
LATER...
OOH-OOH -- RANDOM SECTIONS OF MY COILS KEEP FALLING ASLEEP!
EVERYTHING... FROM MY EYEBALLS DOWN FEELS SO HEAVY.
SIGH PO...
...TRY AND KEEP UP!
HUFF
HUFF
DIDN'T SHIFU SAY, THE JOURNEY IS WITHIN ONESELF... OR IF HE DIDN'T, AND I JUST MADE IT UP, HE SHOULD HAVE! ANYWAY...
...THERE'S A WHOLE LOT MORE OF ME TO NAVIGATE.
THIS IS NO TIME FOR JOKES. WE FACE A GREAT, IF SOMEWHAT UNDEFINED, CHALLENGE.
GOT THAT. I'M JUST FACING IT AT MY OWN SWEET PACE.
SOMETIMES, PO, FOR A DRAGON WARRIOR... I CAN'T HELP BUT FEEL YOU LACK THE NECESSARY FIRE.
DON'T TAKE IT PERSONALLY, PO. SHE'S FIGHTING THIS TOO. AND IT'S MAKING HER IRRITABLE.

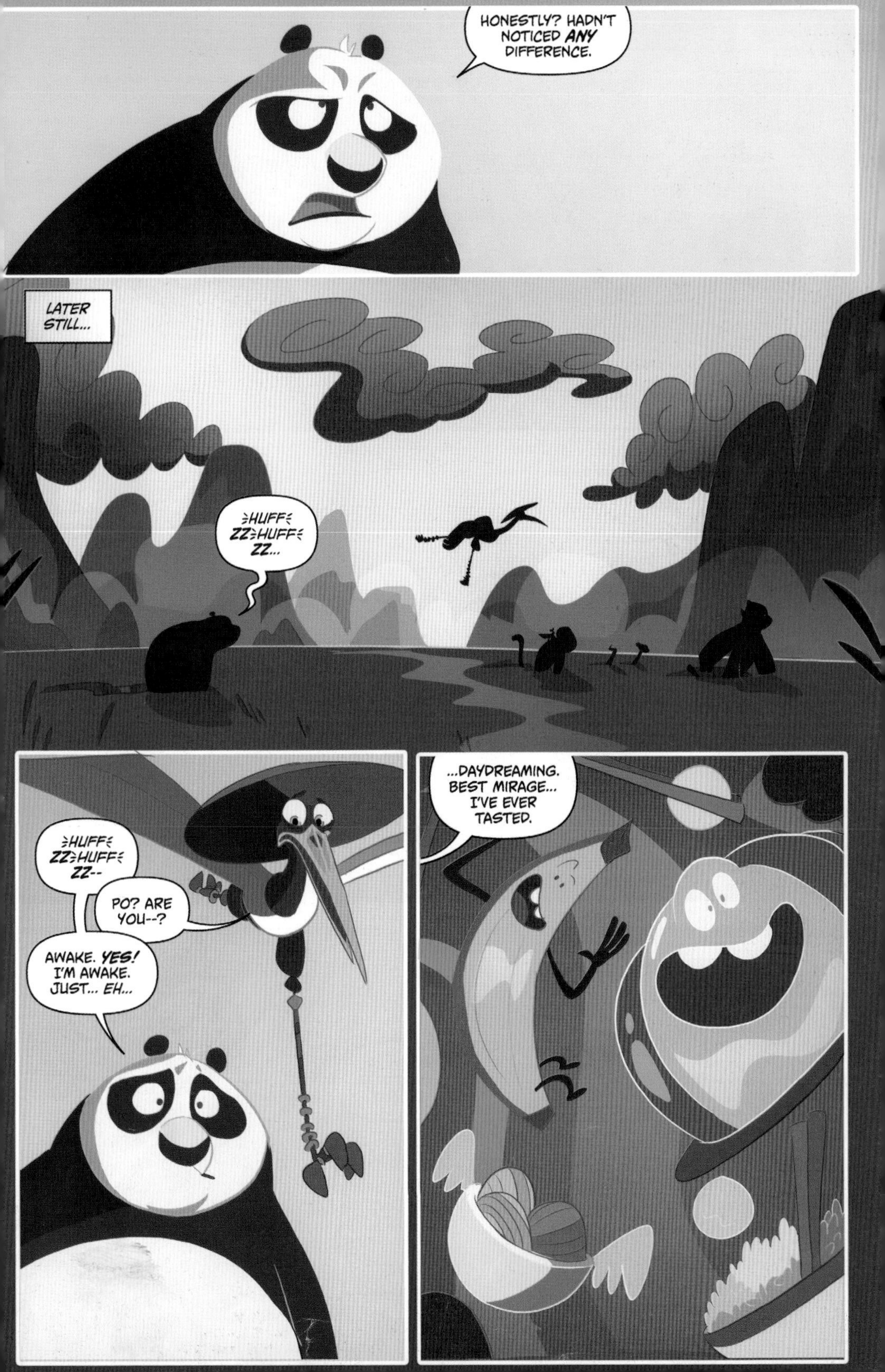
HONESTLY? HADN'T NOTICED ANY DIFFERENCE.
LATER STILL...
HUFF ZZ HUFF ZZ...
HUFF ZZ HUFF ZZ--
PO? ARE YOU--?
AWAKE. YES! I'M AWAKE. JUST... EH...
...DAYDREAMING. BEST MIRAGE... I'VE EVER TASTED.

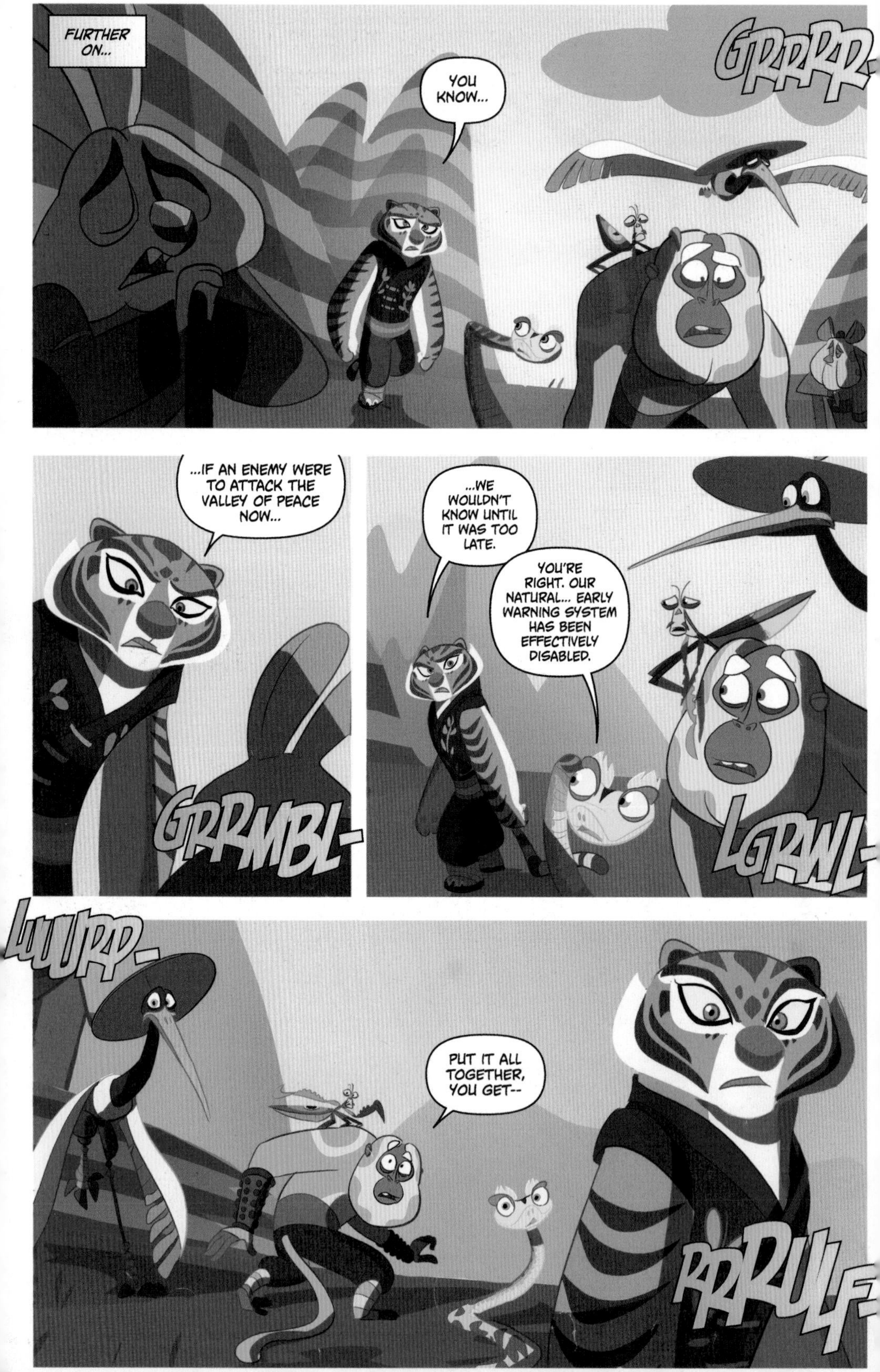
FURTHER ON...
YOU KNOW...
GRRRR-
...IF AN ENEMY WERE TO ATTACK THE VALLEY OF PEACE NOW...
GRRMBL-
...WE WOULDN'T KNOW UNTIL IT WAS TOO LATE.
YOU'RE RIGHT. OUR NATURAL... EARLY WARNING SYSTEM HAS BEEN EFFECTIVELY DISABLED.
LGRWL-
LUUURP-
PUT IT ALL TOGETHER, YOU GET--
RRRULF-

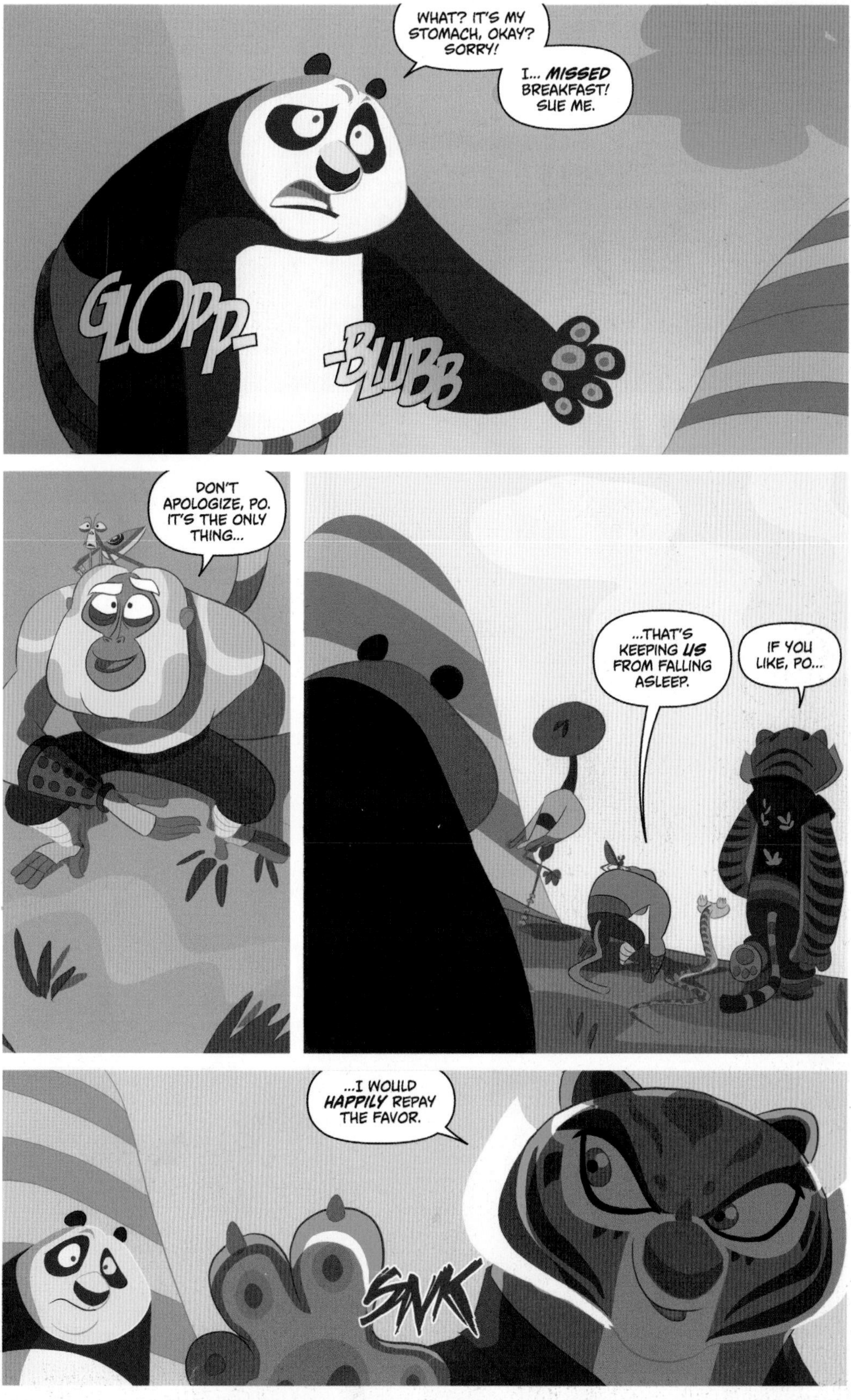
WHAT? IT'S MY STOMACH, OKAY? SORRY!
I... ***MISSED*** BREAKFAST! SUE ME.
GLOPP-
-BLUBB
DON'T APOLOGIZE, PO. IT'S THE ONLY THING...
...THAT'S KEEPING ***US*** FROM FALLING ASLEEP.
IF YOU LIKE, PO...
...I WOULD ***HAPPILY*** REPAY THE FAVOR.
SNK

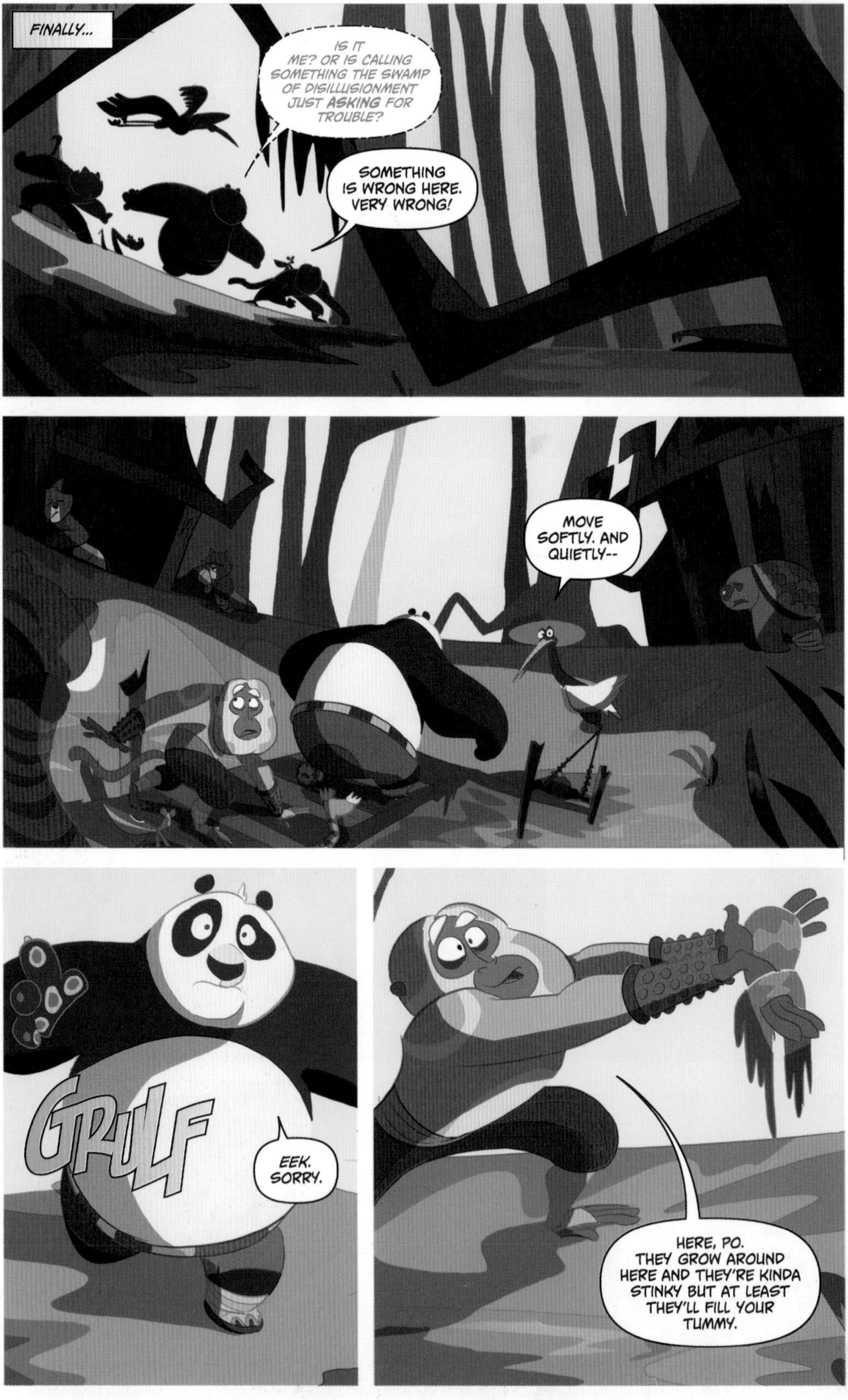
FINALLY...
IS IT ME? OR IS CALLING SOMETHING THE SWAMP OF DISILLUSIONMENT JUST ASKING FOR TROUBLE?
SOMETHING IS WRONG HERE. VERY WRONG!
MOVE SOFTLY. AND QUIETLY--
GRULF
EEK. SORRY.
HERE, PO. THEY GROW AROUND HERE AND THEY'RE KINDA STINKY BUT AT LEAST THEY'LL FILL YOUR TUMMY.

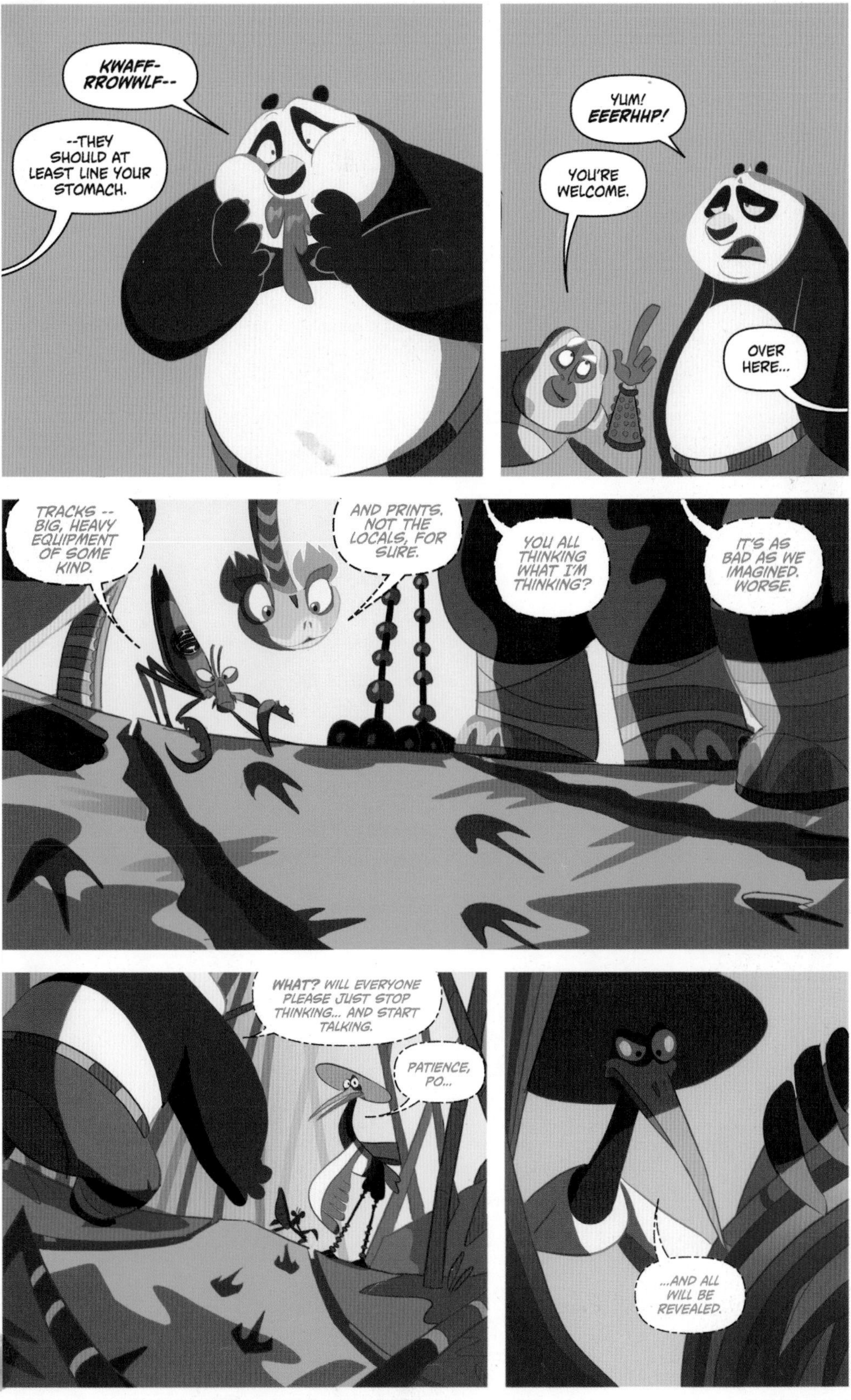
KWAFF-RROWWLF--
--THEY SHOULD AT LEAST LINE YOUR STOMACH.
YUM! EEERHHP!
YOU'RE WELCOME.
OVER HERE...
TRACKS -- BIG, HEAVY EQUIPMENT OF SOME KIND.
AND PRINTS. NOT THE LOCALS, FOR SURE.
YOU ALL THINKING WHAT I'M THINKING?
IT'S AS BAD AS WE IMAGINED. WORSE.
WHAT? WILL EVERYONE PLEASE JUST STOP THINKING... AND START TALKING.
PATIENCE, PO...
...AND ALL WILL BE REVEALED.

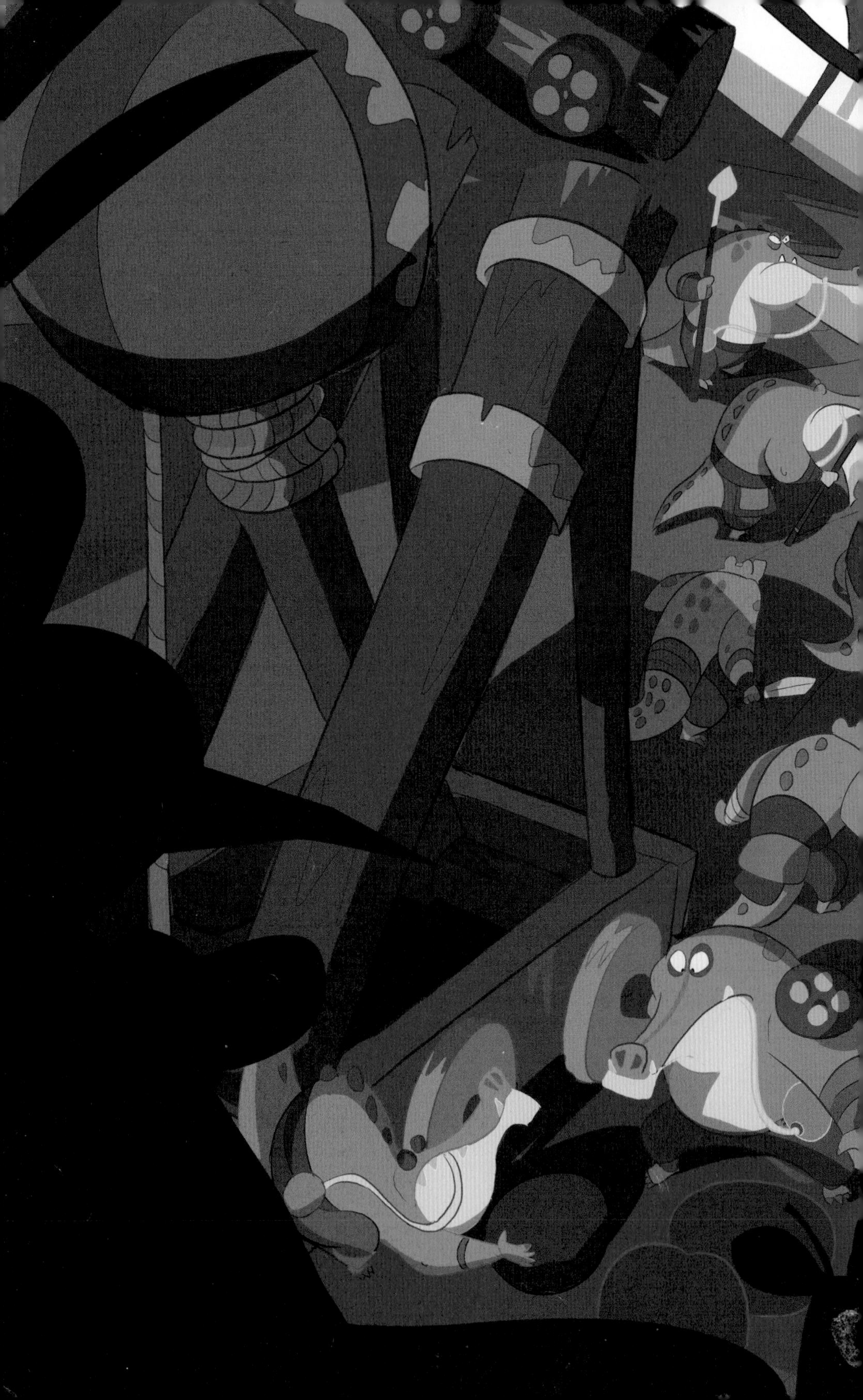

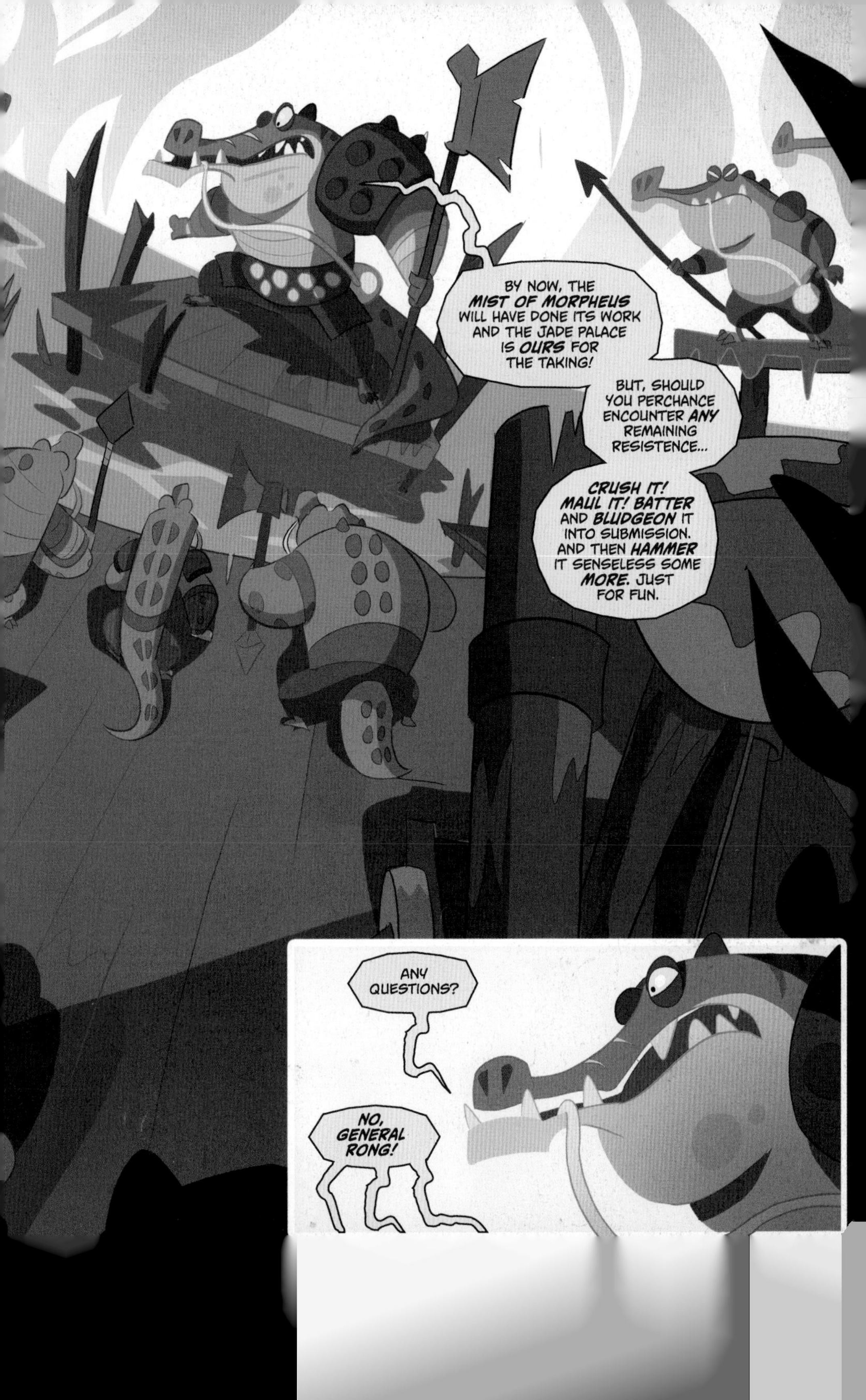
BY NOW, THE MIST OF MORPHEUS WILL HAVE DONE ITS WORK AND THE JADE PALACE IS OURS FOR THE TAKING!
BUT, SHOULD YOU PERCHANCE ENCOUNTER ANY REMAINING RESISTENCE...
CRUSH IT! MAUL IT! BATTER AND BLUDGEON IT INTO SUBMISSION. AND THEN HAMMER IT SENSELESS SOME MORE. JUST FOR FUN.
ANY QUESTIONS?
NO, GENERAL RONG!

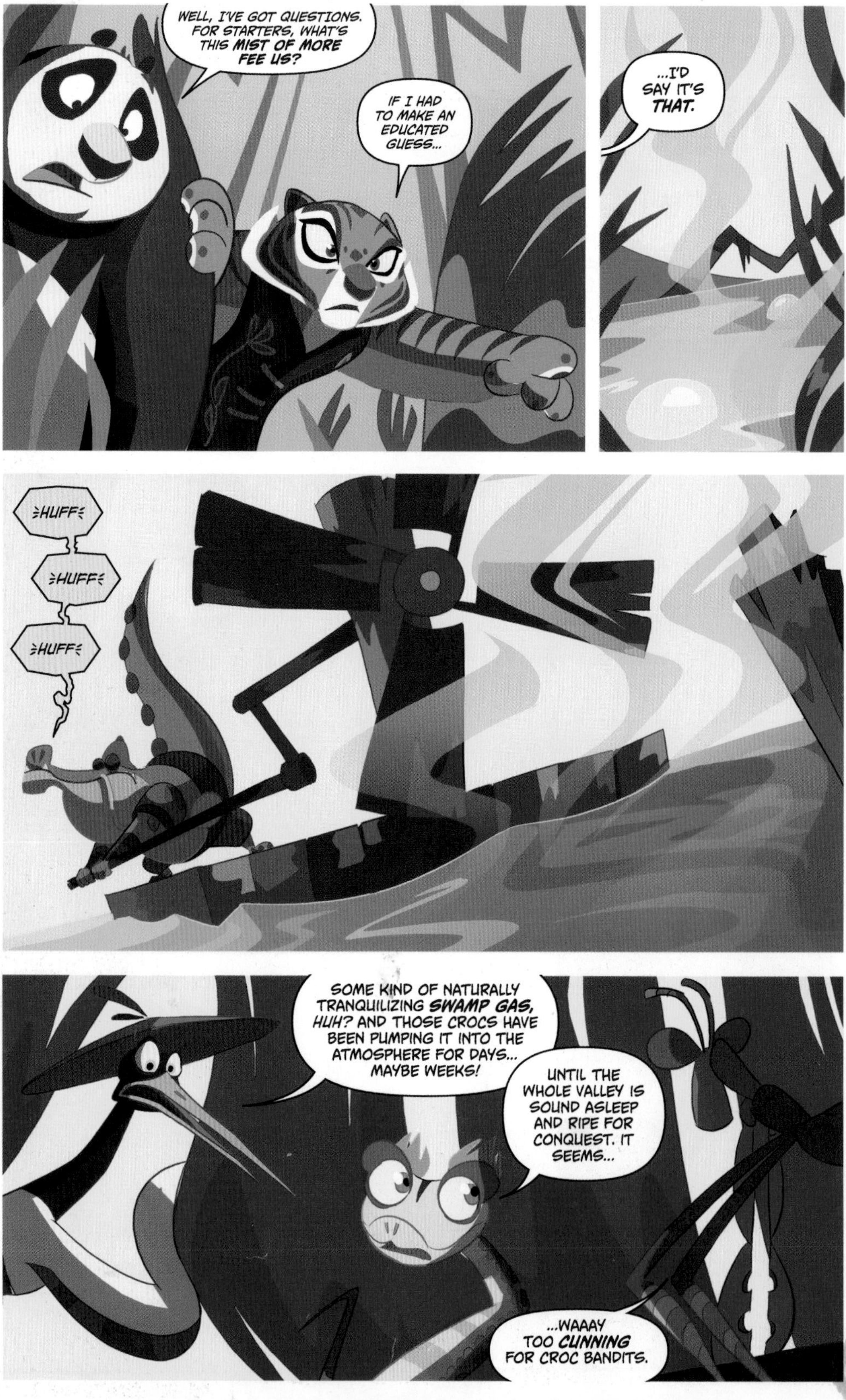
WELL, I'VE GOT QUESTIONS. FOR STARTERS, WHAT'S THIS MIST OF MORE FEE US?
IF I HAD TO MAKE AN EDUCATED GUESS...
...I'D SAY IT'S THAT.
HUFF
HUFF
HUFF
SOME KIND OF NATURALLY TRANQUILIZING SWAMP GAS, HUH? AND THOSE CROCS HAVE BEEN PUMPING IT INTO THE ATMOSPHERE FOR DAYS... MAYBE WEEKS!
UNTIL THE WHOLE VALLEY IS SOUND ASLEEP AND RIPE FOR CONQUEST. IT SEEMS...
...WAAAY TOO CUNNING FOR CROC BANDITS.

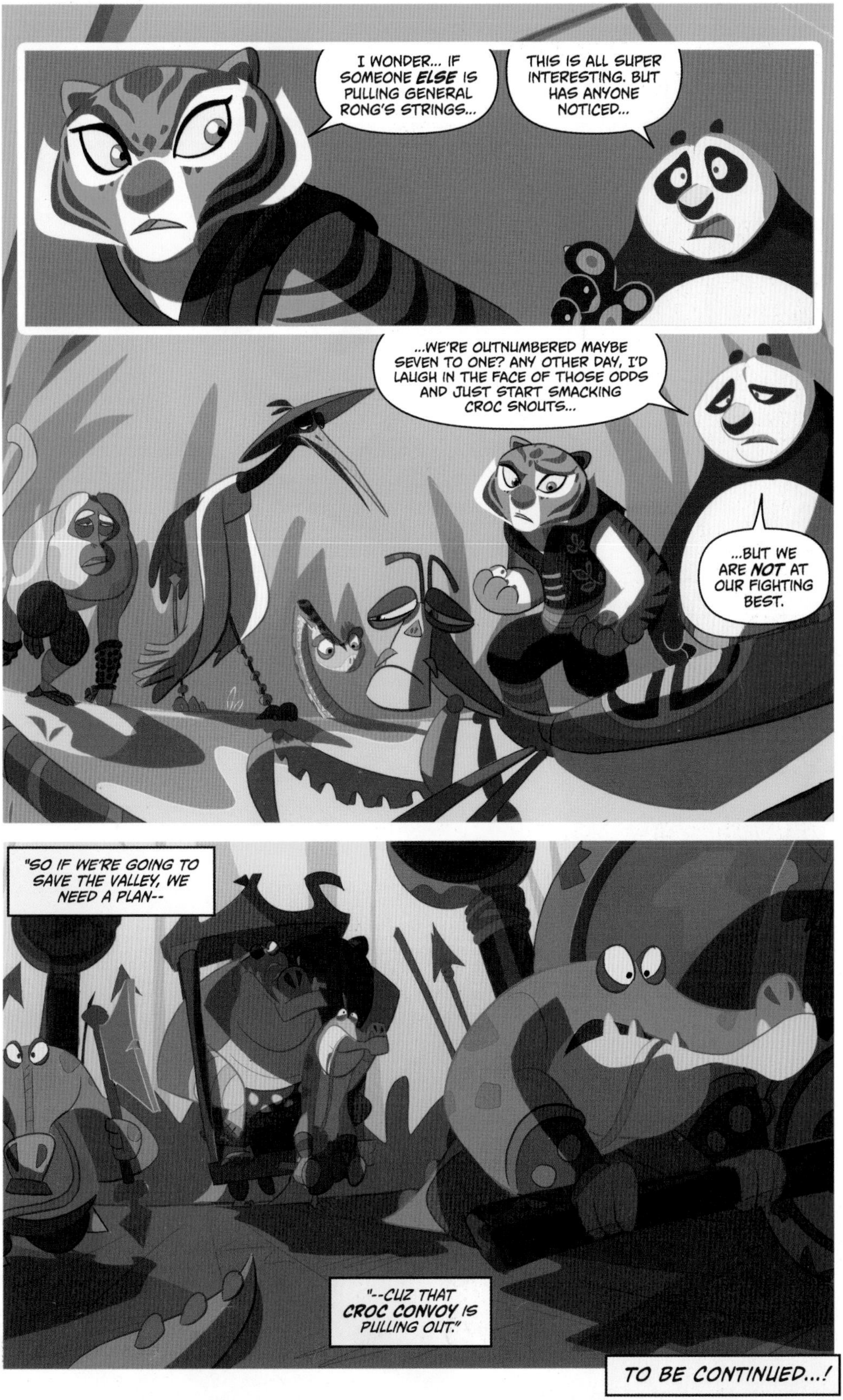
I WONDER... IF SOMEONE *ELSE* IS PULLING GENERAL RONG'S STRINGS...
THIS IS ALL SUPER INTERESTING. BUT HAS ANYONE NOTICED...
...WE'RE OUTNUMBERED MAYBE SEVEN TO ONE? ANY OTHER DAY, I'D LAUGH IN THE FACE OF THOSE ODDS AND JUST START SMACKING CROC SNOUTS...
...BUT WE ARE ***NOT*** AT OUR FIGHTING BEST.
"SO IF WE'RE GOING TO SAVE THE VALLEY, WE NEED A PLAN--
"--CUZ THAT ***CROC CONVOY*** IS PULLING OUT."
TO BE CONTINUED...!

# CHAPTER 2

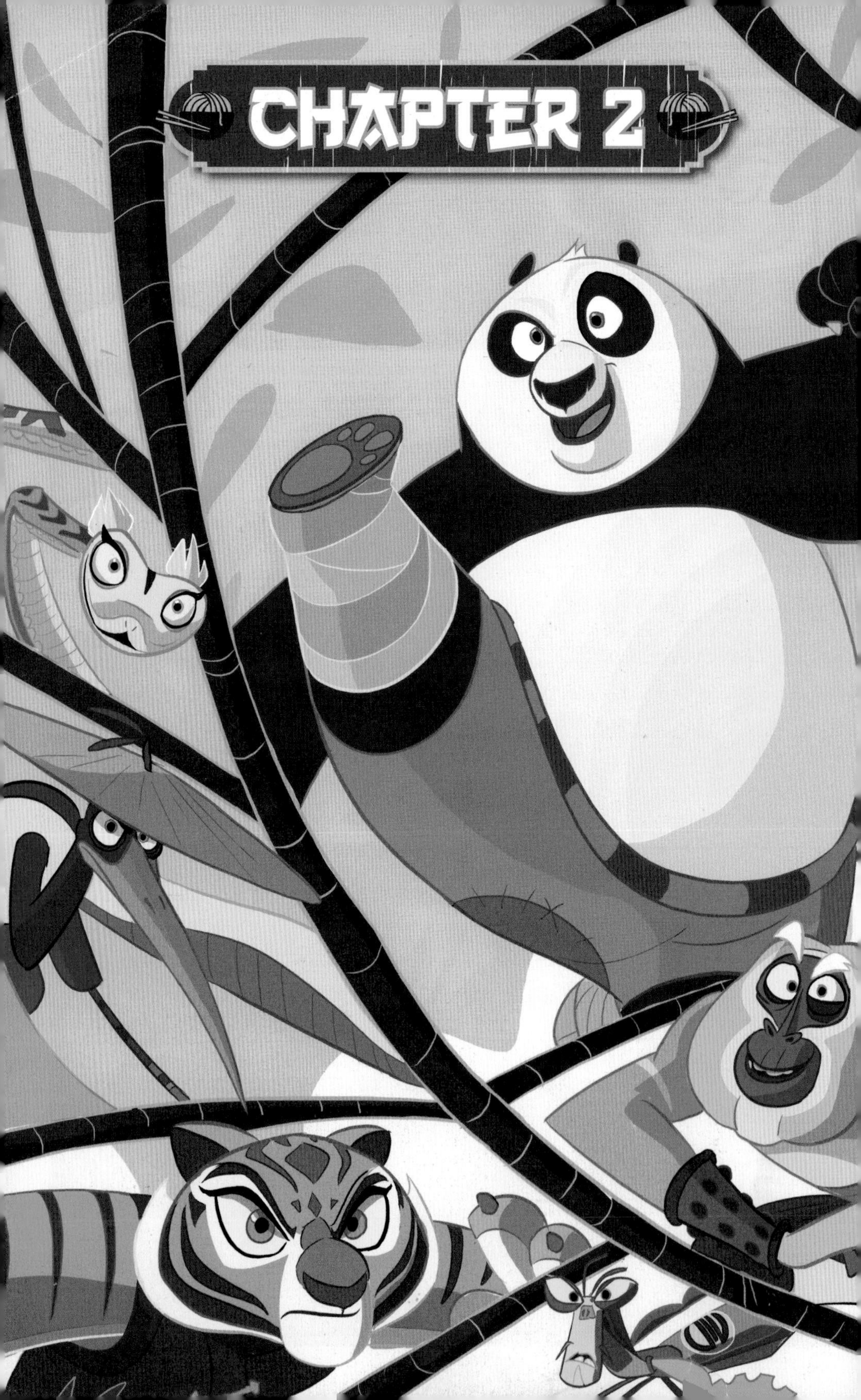

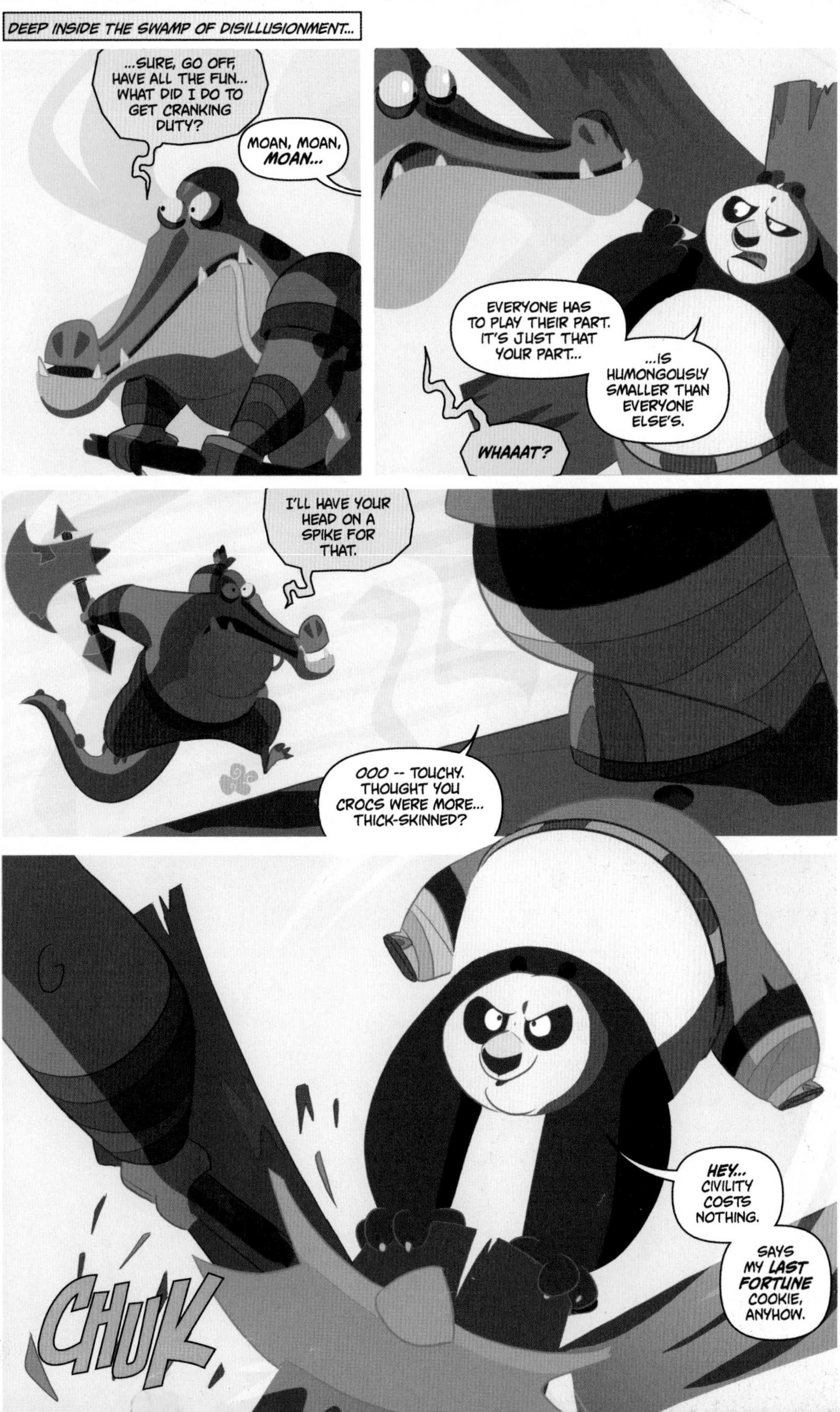
DEEP INSIDE THE SWAMP OF DISILLUSIONMENT...
...SURE, GO OFF, HAVE ALL THE FUN... WHAT DID I DO TO GET CRANKING DUTY?
MOAN, MOAN, MOAN...
EVERYONE HAS TO PLAY THEIR PART. IT'S JUST THAT YOUR PART...
...IS HUMONGOUSLY SMALLER THAN EVERYONE ELSE'S.
WHAAAT?
I'LL HAVE YOUR HEAD ON A SPIKE FOR THAT.
OOO -- TOUCHY. THOUGHT YOU CROCS WERE MORE... THICK-SKINNED?
CHUK
HEY... CIVILITY COSTS NOTHING.
SAYS MY LAST FORTUNE COOKIE, ANYHOW.

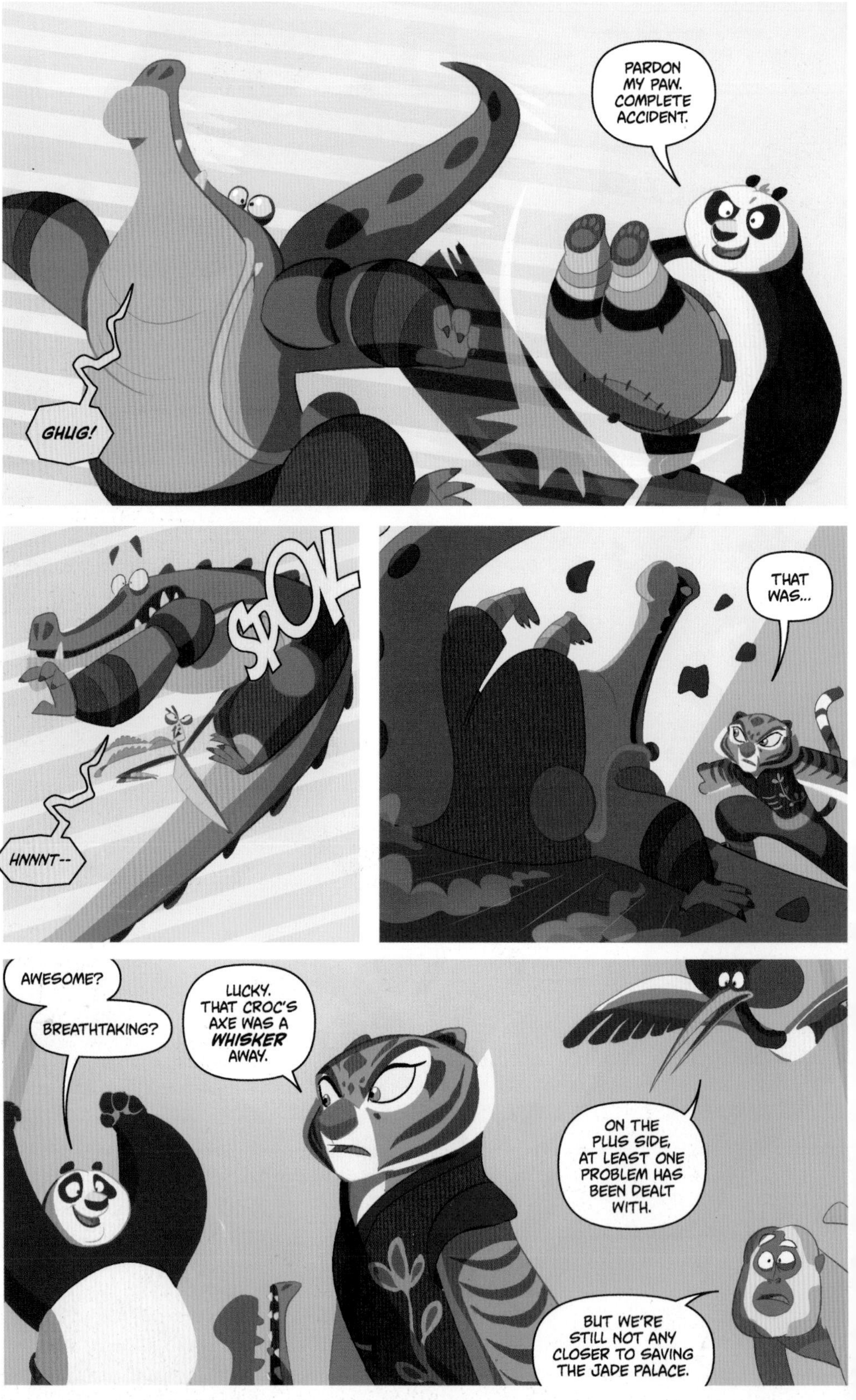
PARDON MY PAW. COMPLETE ACCIDENT.
GHUG!
SPOK
HNNNT--
THAT WAS...
AWESOME?
BREATHTAKING?
LUCKY. THAT CROC'S AXE WAS A **WHISKER** AWAY.
ON THE PLUS SIDE, AT LEAST ONE PROBLEM HAS BEEN DEALT WITH.
BUT WE'RE STILL NOT ANY CLOSER TO SAVING THE JADE PALACE.

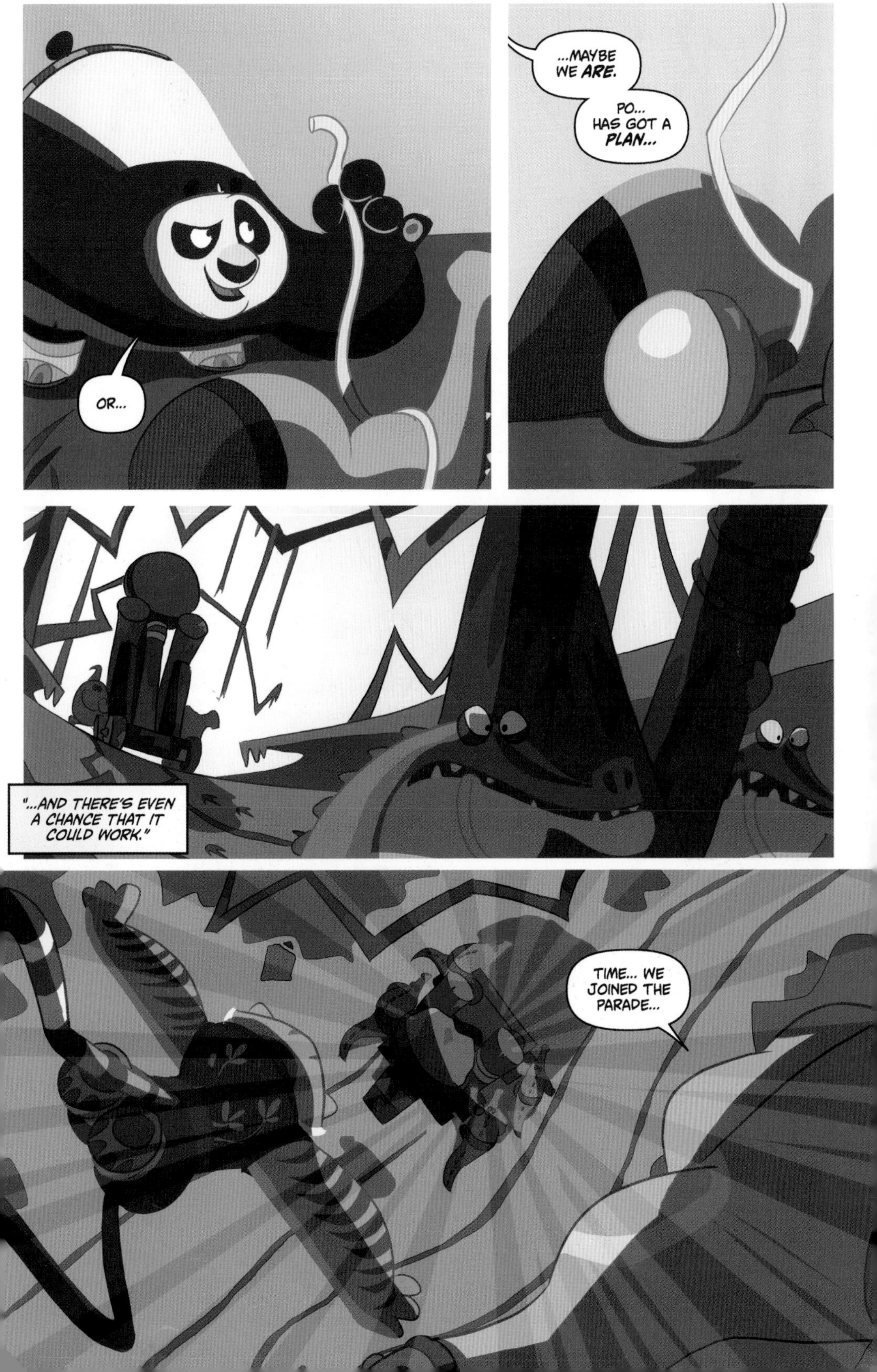
OR...
...MAYBE WE ARE.
PO... HAS GOT A PLAN...
"...AND THERE'S EVEN A CHANCE THAT IT COULD WORK."
TIME... WE JOINED THE PARADE...

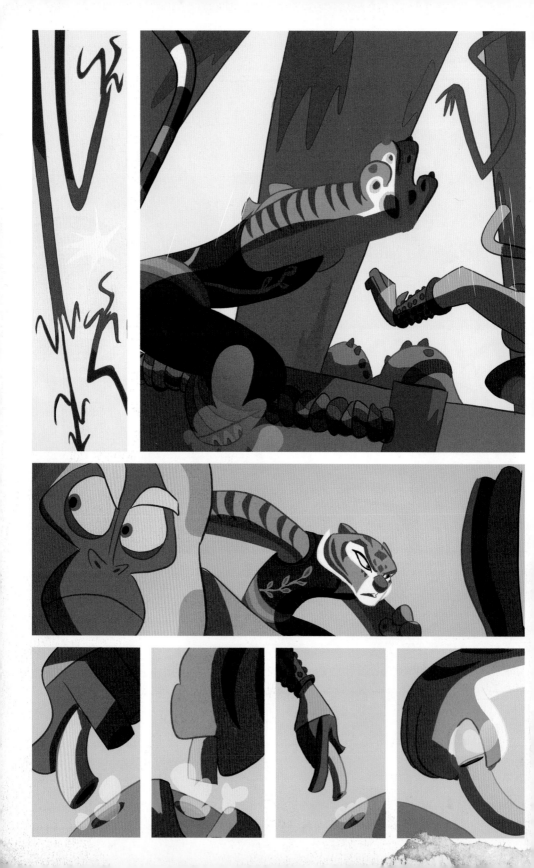

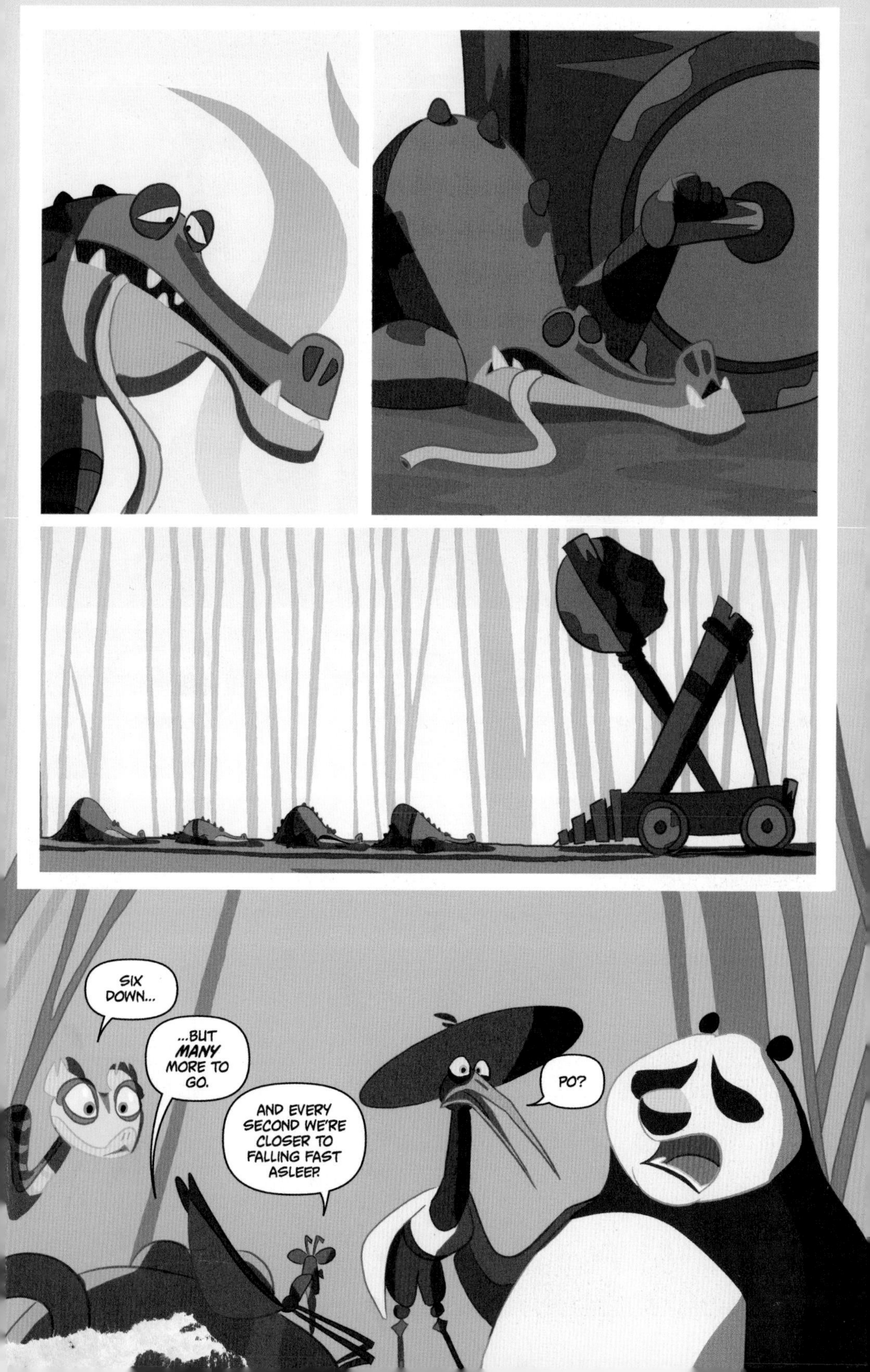
SIX DOWN...
...BUT *MANY* MORE TO GO.
AND EVERY SECOND WE'RE CLOSER TO FALLING FAST ASLEEP.
PO?

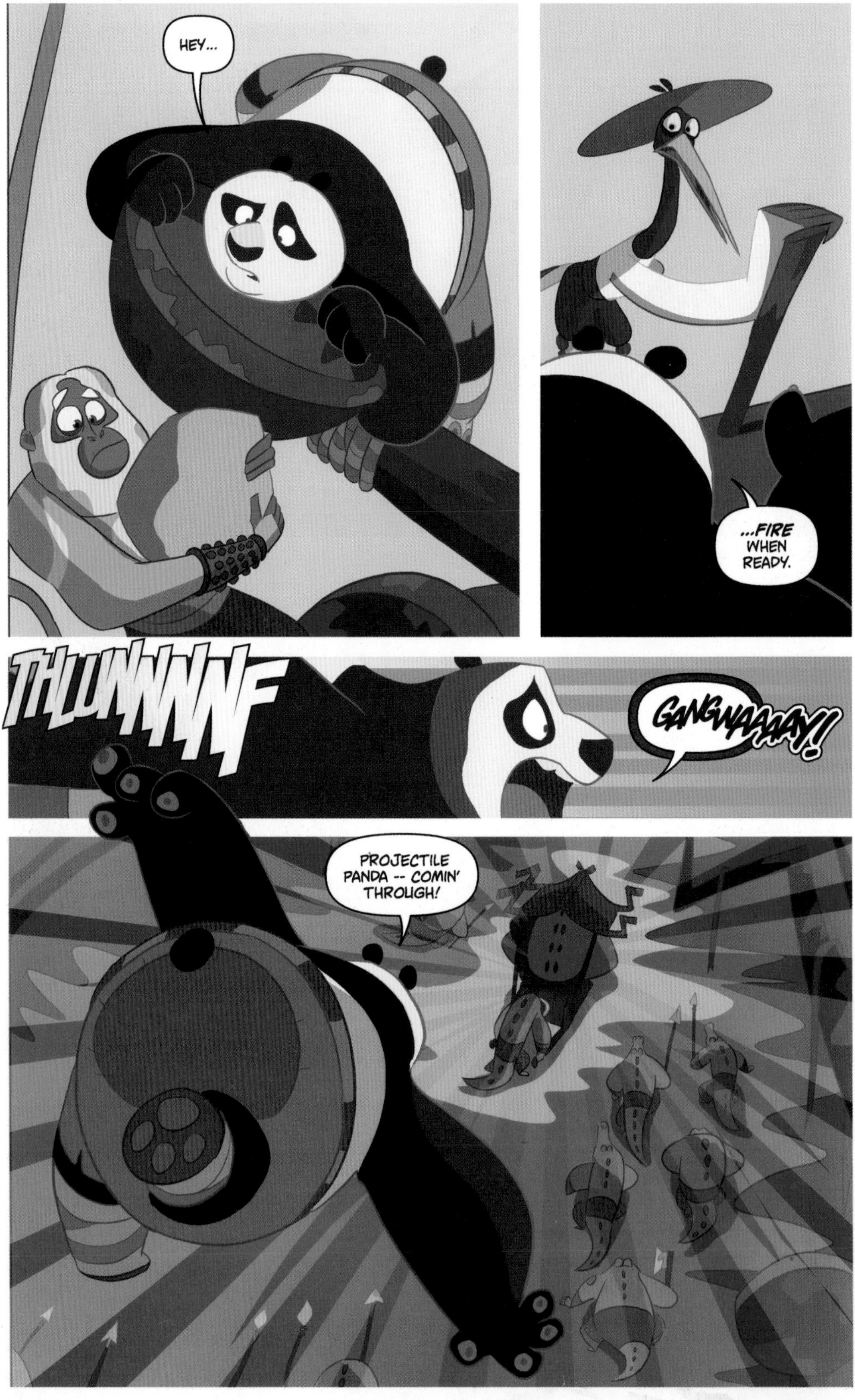
HEY...
...FIRE WHEN READY.
THLUNNNNF
GANGWAAAAAY!
PROJECTILE PANDA -- COMIN' THROUGH!

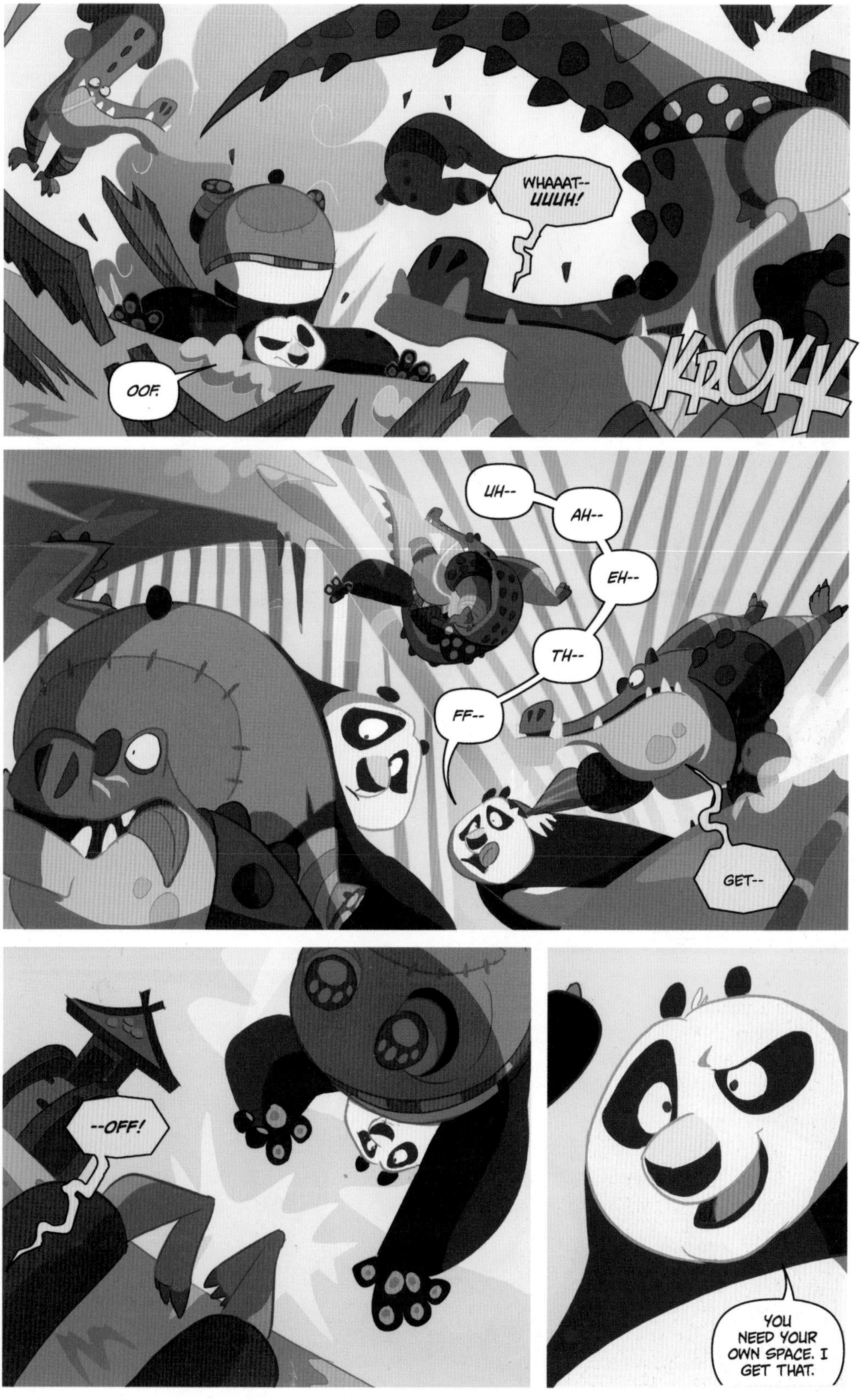
WHAAAT--
UUUH!
OOF.
KROKK
UH--
AH--
EH--
TH--
FF--
GET--
--OFF!
YOU NEED YOUR OWN SPACE. I GET THAT.

WHOA -- OKAY. TOUCHED A SORE SPOT THERE.

DRAGON WARRIOR -- *FAH.* YOU HAVE NO IDEA, NONE AT ALL...

...THE *GREAT TERROR* THAT IS COMING.

TALK IS CHEAP, RONG. BUT BY ALL MEANS KEEP SNAPPIN' THEM SCALY JAWS O' YOURS.

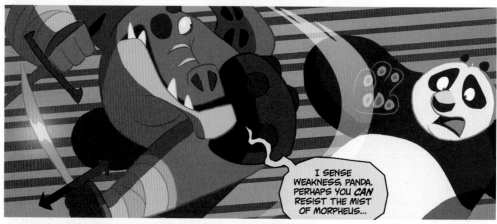

I SENSE WEAKNESS, PANDA. PERHAPS YOU *CAN* RESIST THE MIST OF MORPHEUS...

...BUT FOR HOW LONG?

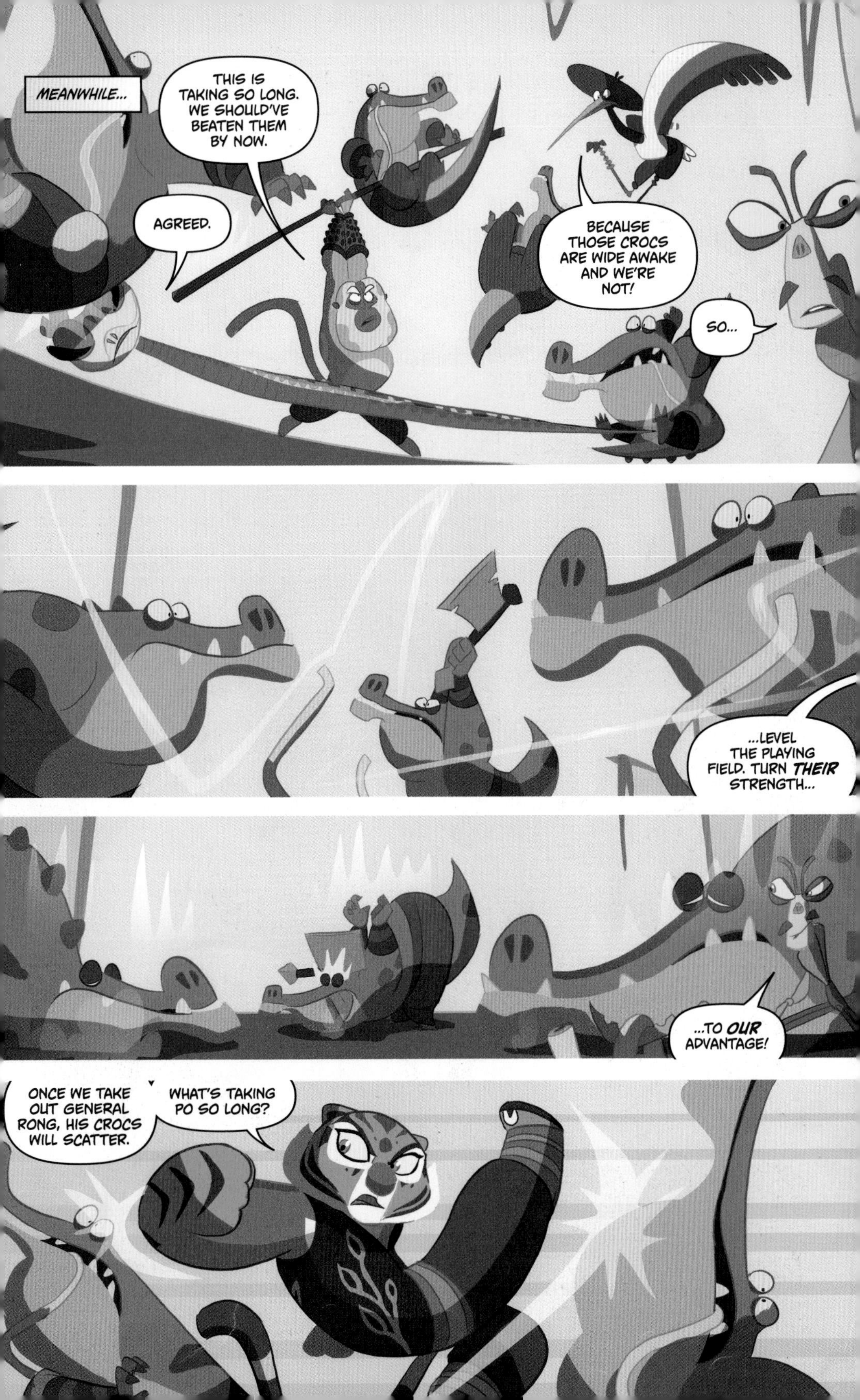
MEANWHILE...
THIS IS TAKING SO LONG. WE SHOULD'VE BEATEN THEM BY NOW.
AGREED.
BECAUSE THOSE CROCS ARE WIDE AWAKE AND WE'RE NOT!
SO...
...LEVEL THE PLAYING FIELD. TURN *THEIR* STRENGTH...
...TO *OUR* ADVANTAGE!
ONCE WE TAKE OUT GENERAL RONG, HIS CROCS WILL SCATTER.
WHAT'S TAKING PO SO LONG?

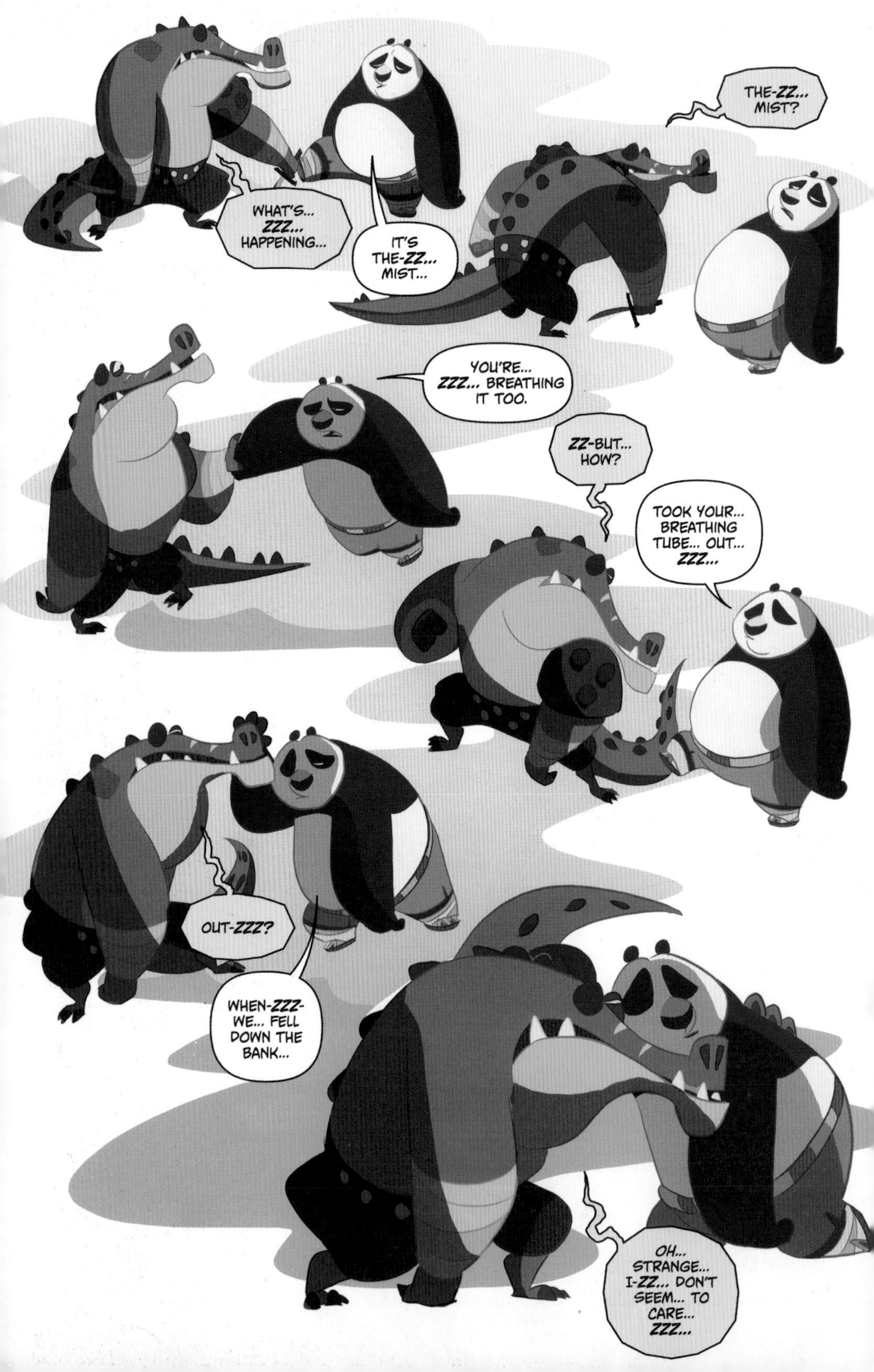
WHAT'S... ZZZ... HAPPENING...
IT'S THE-ZZ... MIST...
THE-ZZ... MIST?
YOU'RE... ZZZ... BREATHING IT TOO.
ZZ-BUT... HOW?
TOOK YOUR... BREATHING TUBE... OUT... ZZZ...
OUT-ZZZ?
WHEN-ZZZ-WE... FELL DOWN THE BANK...
OH... STRANGE... I-ZZ... DON'T SEEM... TO CARE... ZZZ...

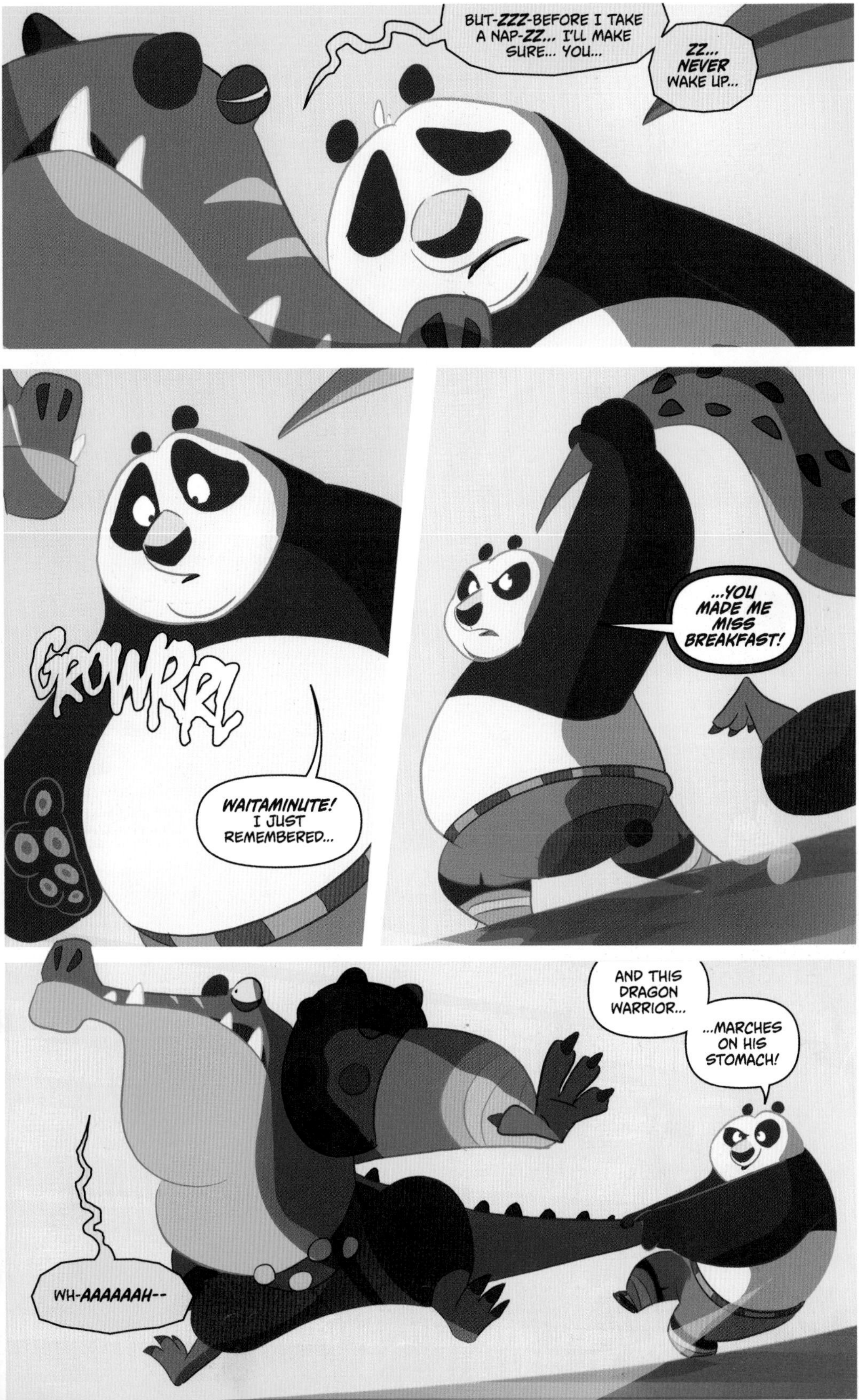
BUT-ZZZ-BEFORE I TAKE A NAP-ZZ... I'LL MAKE SURE... YOU...
ZZ... NEVER WAKE UP...
GROWRRL
WAITAMINUTE! I JUST REMEMBERED...
...YOU MADE ME MISS BREAKFAST!
AND THIS DRAGON WARRIOR...
...MARCHES ON HIS STOMACH!
WH-AAAAAAH--

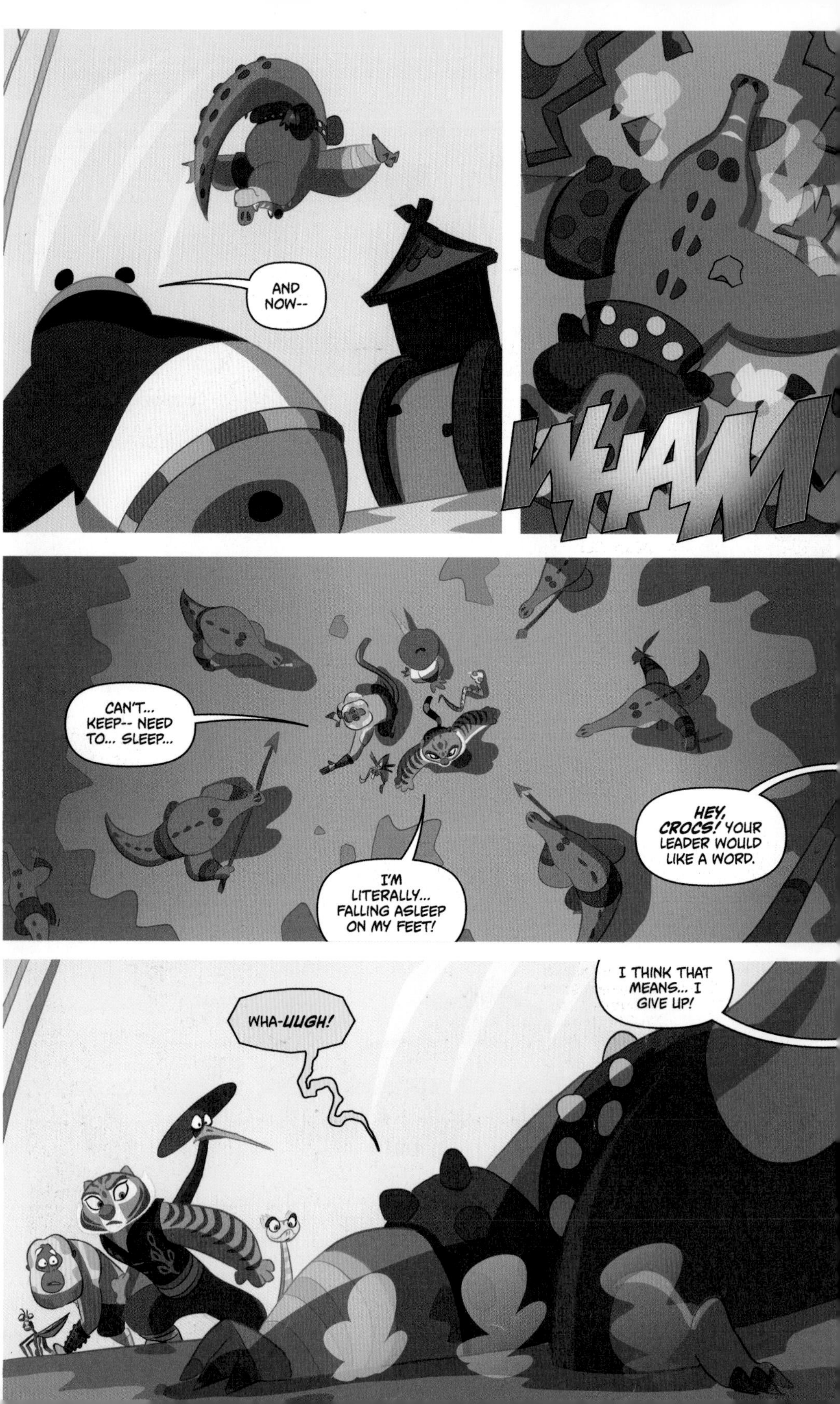
AND NOW--
WHAM
CAN'T... KEEP-- NEED TO... SLEEP...
I'M LITERALLY... FALLING ASLEEP ON MY FEET!
HEY, CROCS! YOUR LEADER WOULD LIKE A WORD.
WHA-UUGH!
I THINK THAT MEANS... I GIVE UP!

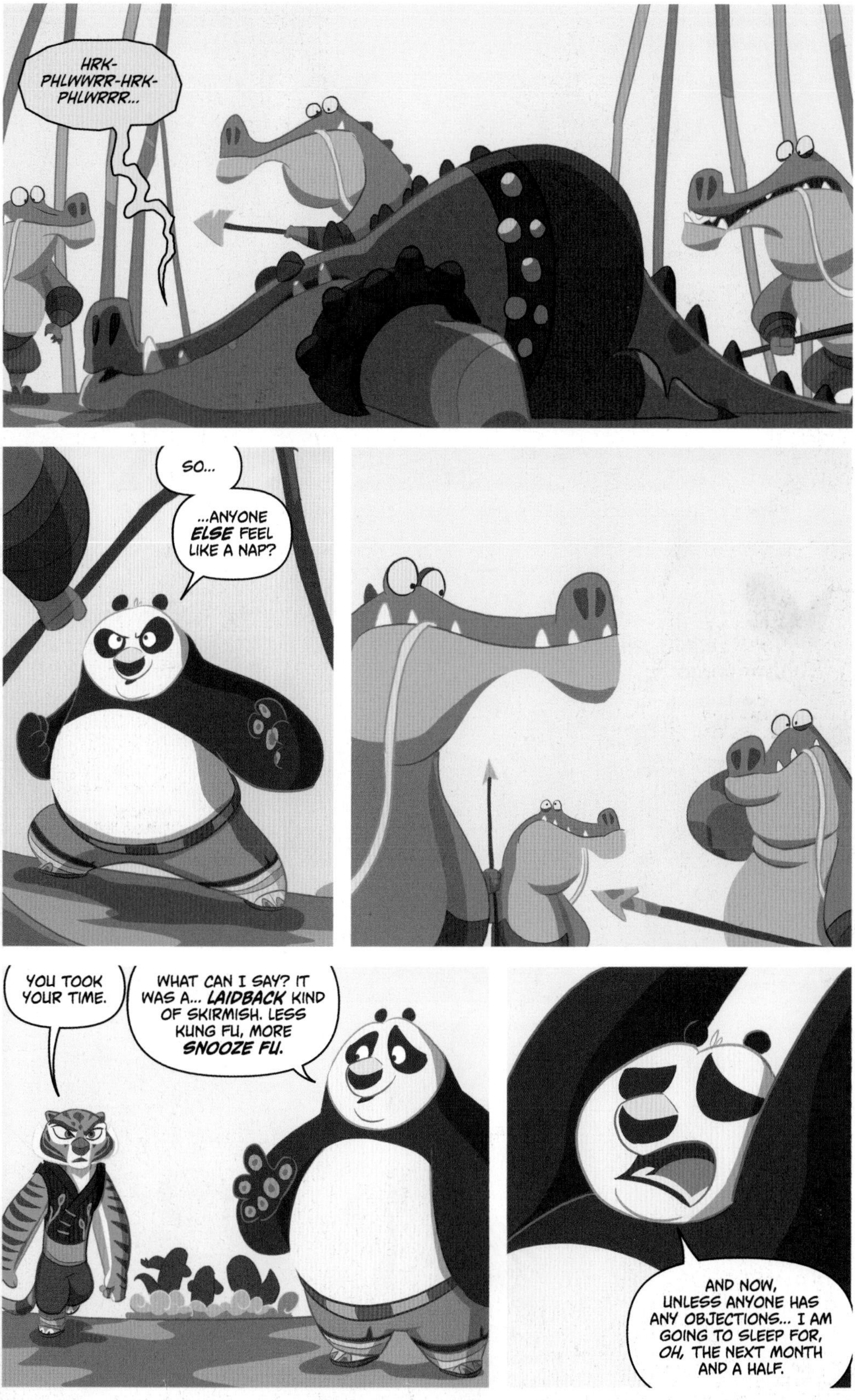
HRK-PHLWWRR-HRK-PHLWRRR...
SO...
...ANYONE ELSE FEEL LIKE A NAP?
YOU TOOK YOUR TIME.
WHAT CAN I SAY? IT WAS A... LAIDBACK KIND OF SKIRMISH. LESS KUNG FU, MORE SNOOZE FU.
AND NOW, UNLESS ANYONE HAS ANY OBJECTIONS... I AM GOING TO SLEEP FOR, OH, THE NEXT MONTH AND A HALF.

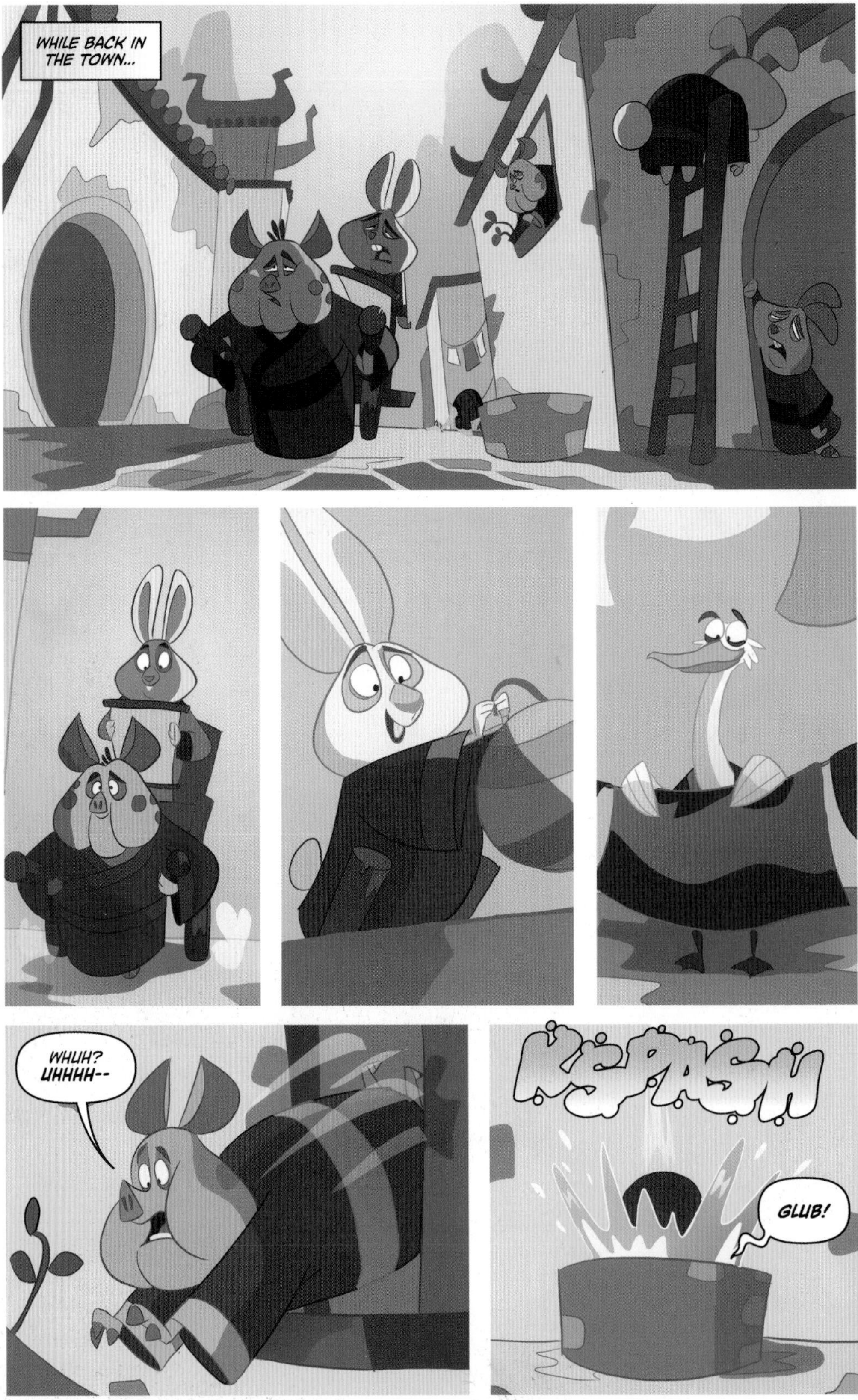
WHILE BACK IN THE TOWN...
WHUH? UHHHH--
KSPASH
GLUB!

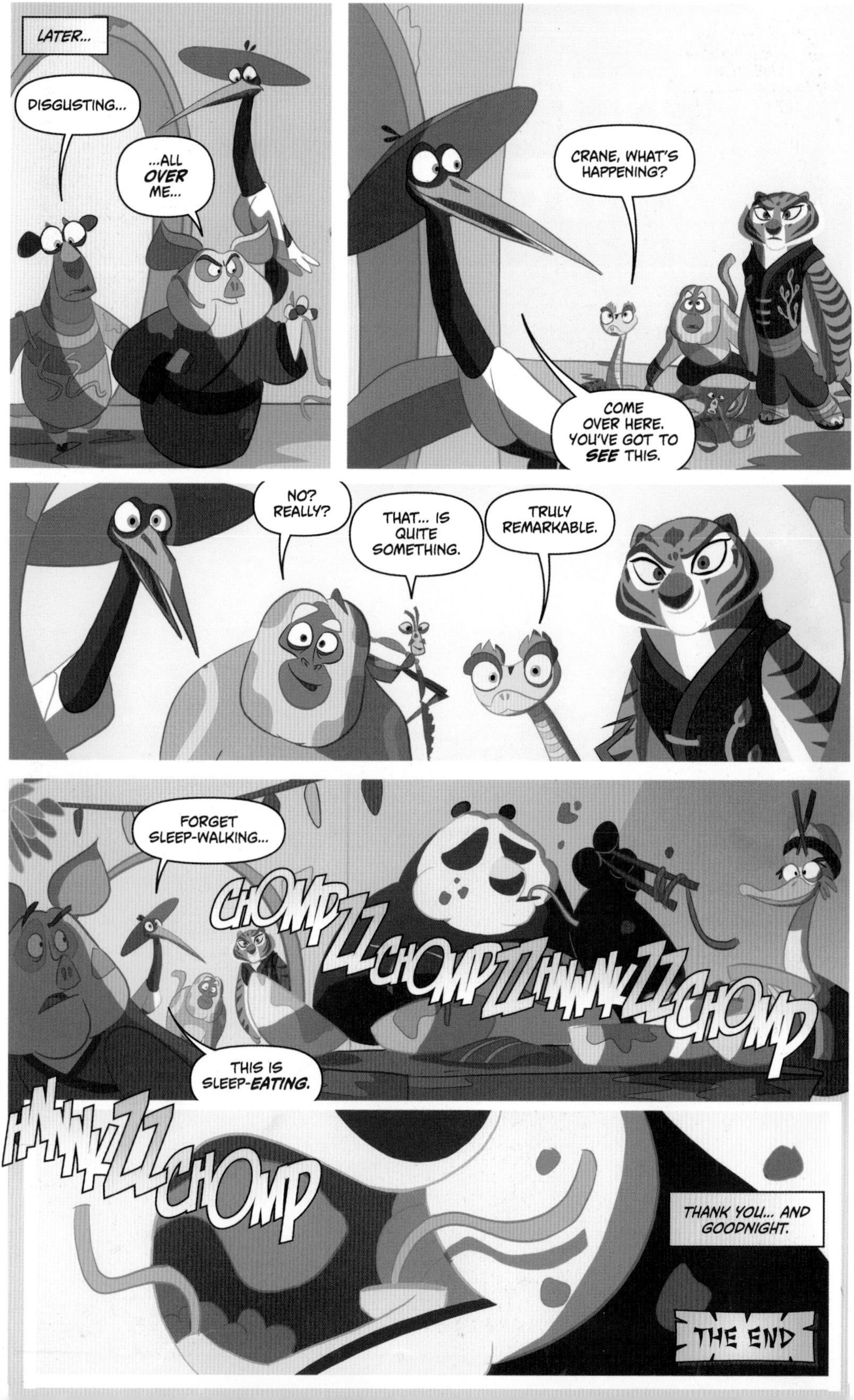
LATER...
DISGUSTING...
...ALL OVER ME...
CRANE, WHAT'S HAPPENING?
COME OVER HERE. YOU'VE GOT TO SEE THIS.
NO? REALLY?
THAT... IS QUITE SOMETHING.
TRULY REMARKABLE.
FORGET SLEEP-WALKING...
CHOMP ZZ CHOMP ZZ HNNNK ZZ CHOMP
THIS IS SLEEP-EATING.
HNNNK ZZ CHOMP
THANK YOU... AND GOODNIGHT.
THE END

# NO REST FOR THE WICKED

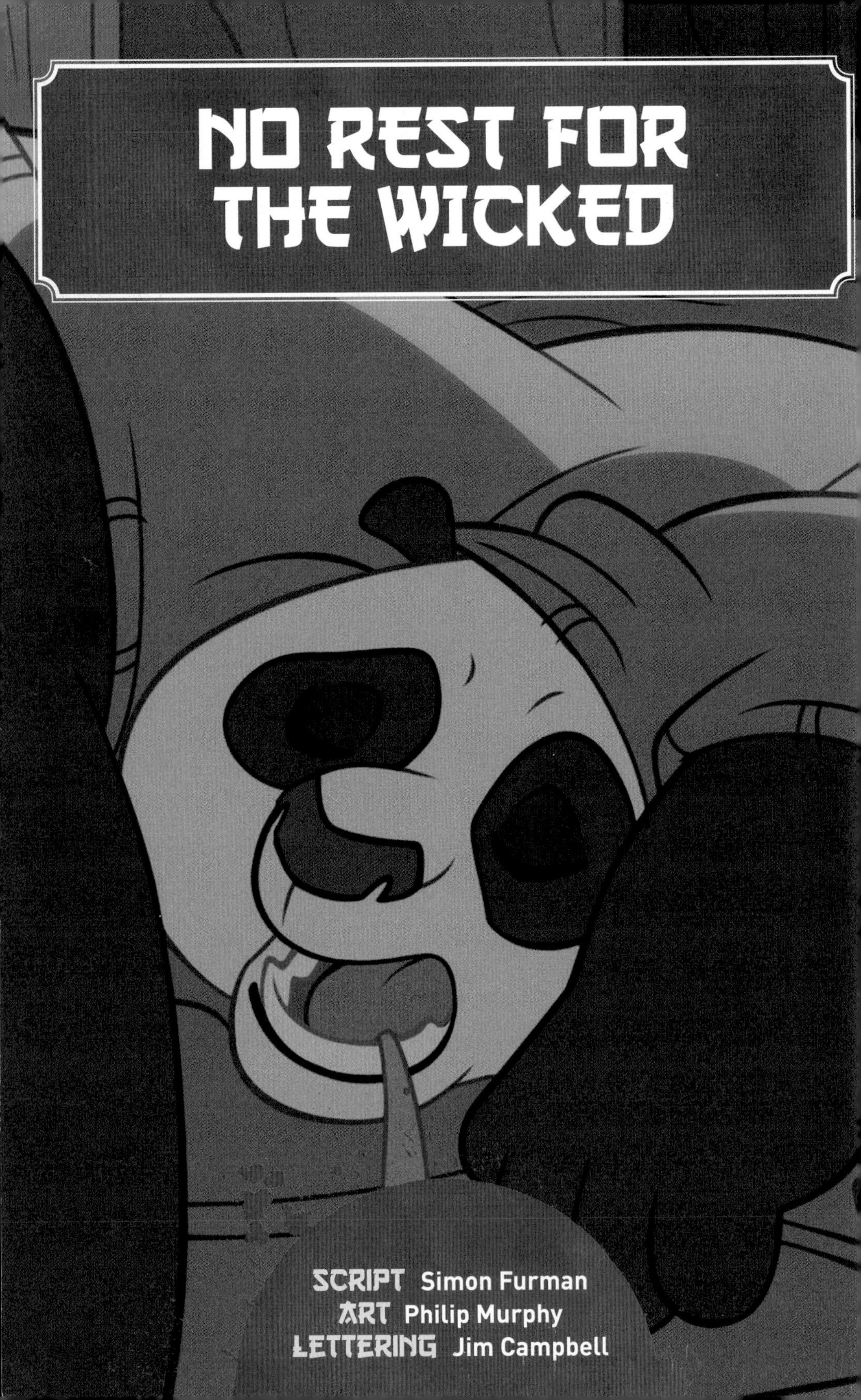

SCRIPT Simon Furman
ART Philip Murphy
LETTERING Jim Campbell

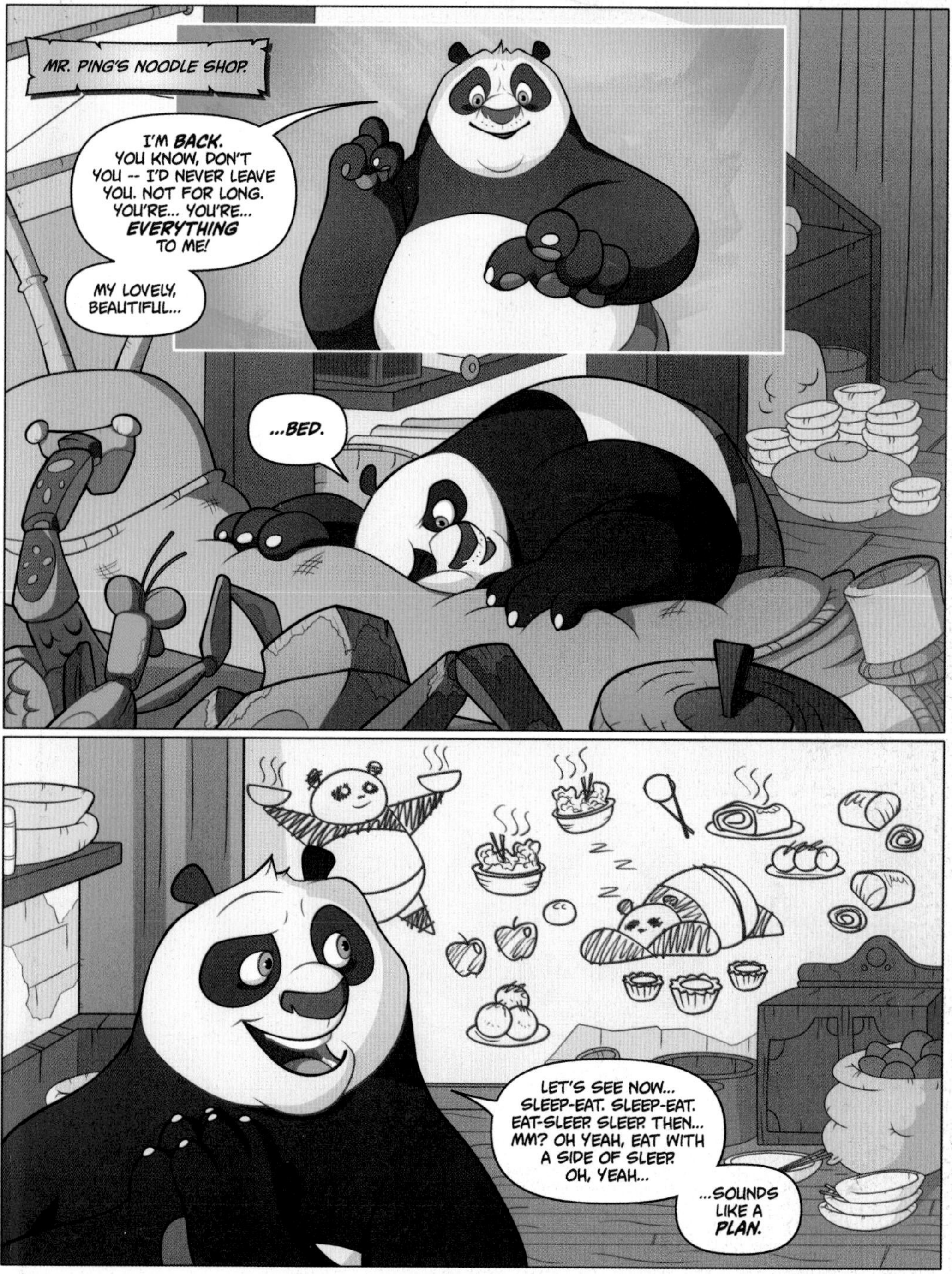
MR. PING'S NOODLE SHOP.
I'M BACK. YOU KNOW, DON'T YOU -- I'D NEVER LEAVE YOU. NOT FOR LONG. YOU'RE... YOU'RE... EVERYTHING TO ME!
MY LOVELY, BEAUTIFUL...
...BED.
LET'S SEE NOW... SLEEP-EAT. SLEEP-EAT. EAT-SLEEP. SLEEP. THEN... MM? OH YEAH, EAT WITH A SIDE OF SLEEP. OH, YEAH...
...SOUNDS LIKE A PLAN.

# NO REST FOR THE WICKED

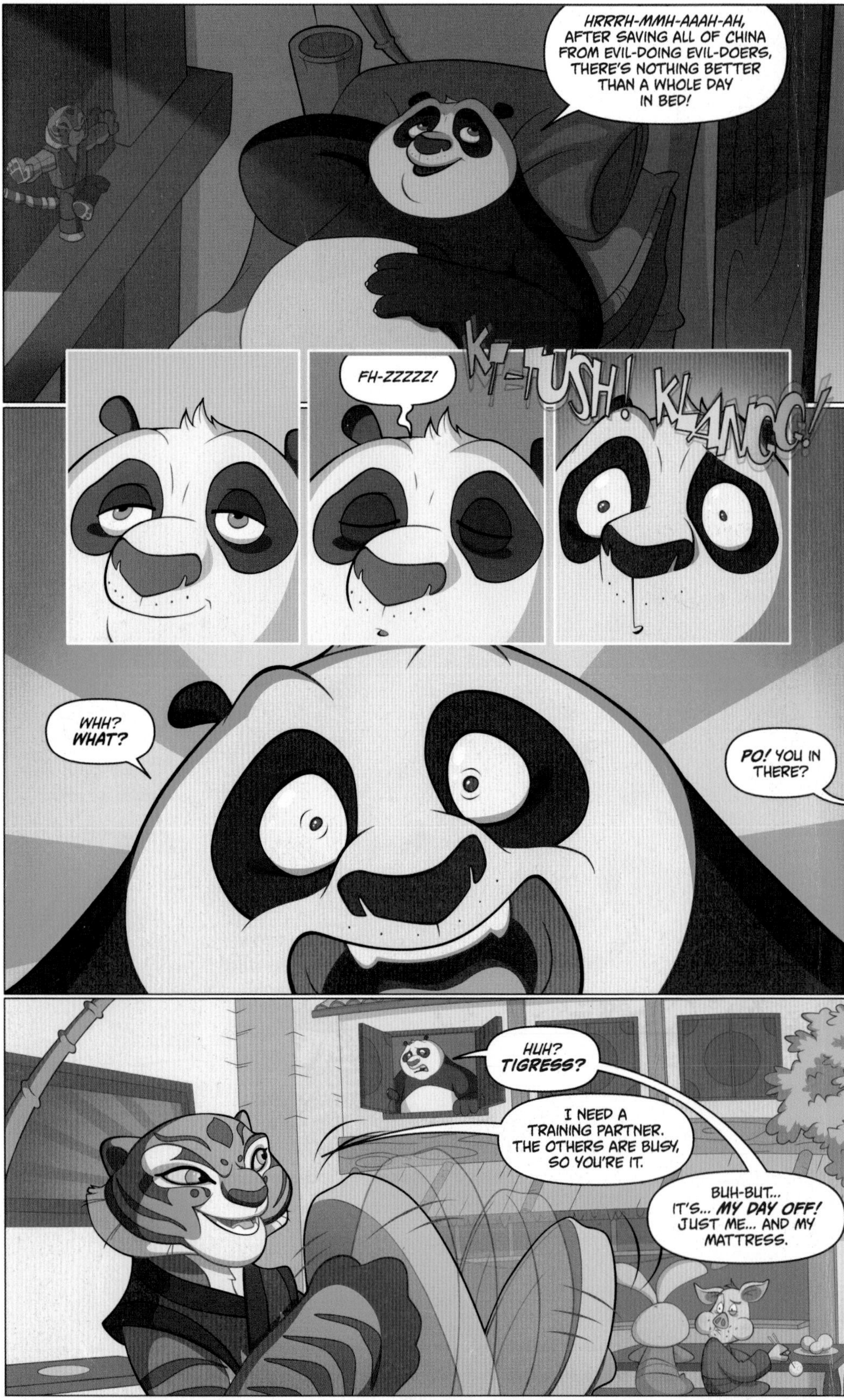

HRRRH-MMH-AAAH-AH, AFTER SAVING ALL OF CHINA FROM EVIL-DOING EVIL-DOERS, THERE'S NOTHING BETTER THAN A WHOLE DAY IN BED!
FH-ZZZZZ!
KI-TUSH! KLANGG!
WHH? WHAT?
PO! YOU IN THERE?
HUH? TIGRESS?
I NEED A TRAINING PARTNER. THE OTHERS ARE BUSY, SO YOU'RE IT.
BUH-BUT... IT'S... MY DAY OFF! JUST ME... AND MY MATTRESS.

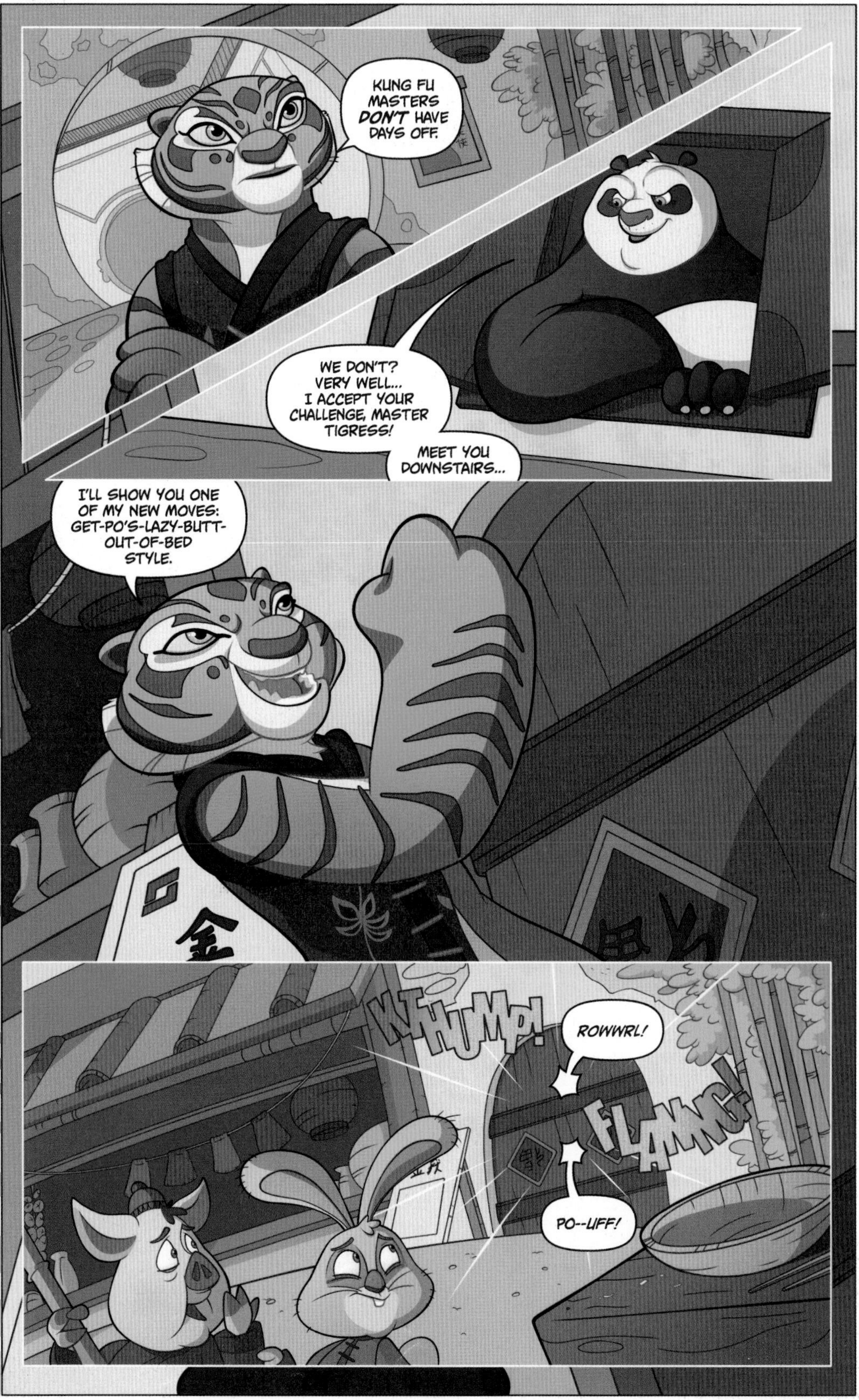
KUNG FU MASTERS DON'T HAVE DAYS OFF.
WE DON'T? VERY WELL... I ACCEPT YOUR CHALLENGE, MASTER TIGRESS!
MEET YOU DOWNSTAIRS...
I'LL SHOW YOU ONE OF MY NEW MOVES: GET-PO'S-LAZY-BUTT-OUT-OF-BED STYLE.
KTHUMP!
ROWWRL!
FLANNG!
PO--UFF!

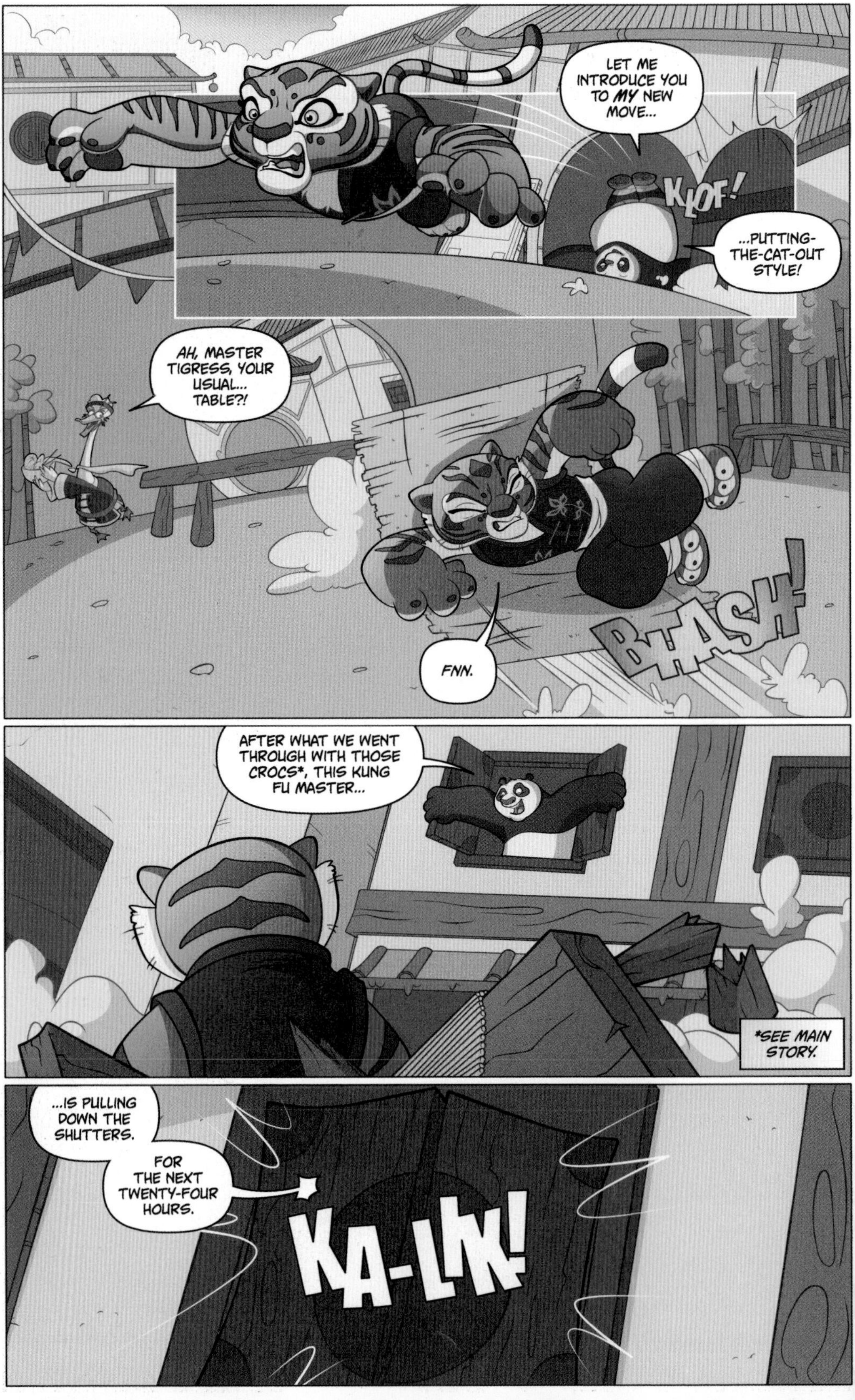
LET ME INTRODUCE YOU TO MY NEW MOVE...
KLOF!
...PUTTING-THE-CAT-OUT STYLE!
AH, MASTER TIGRESS, YOUR USUAL... TABLE?!
FNN.
BHASH!
AFTER WHAT WE WENT THROUGH WITH THOSE CROCS*, THIS KUNG FU MASTER...
*SEE MAIN STORY.
...IS PULLING DOWN THE SHUTTERS.
FOR THE NEXT TWENTY-FOUR HOURS.
KA-LIK!

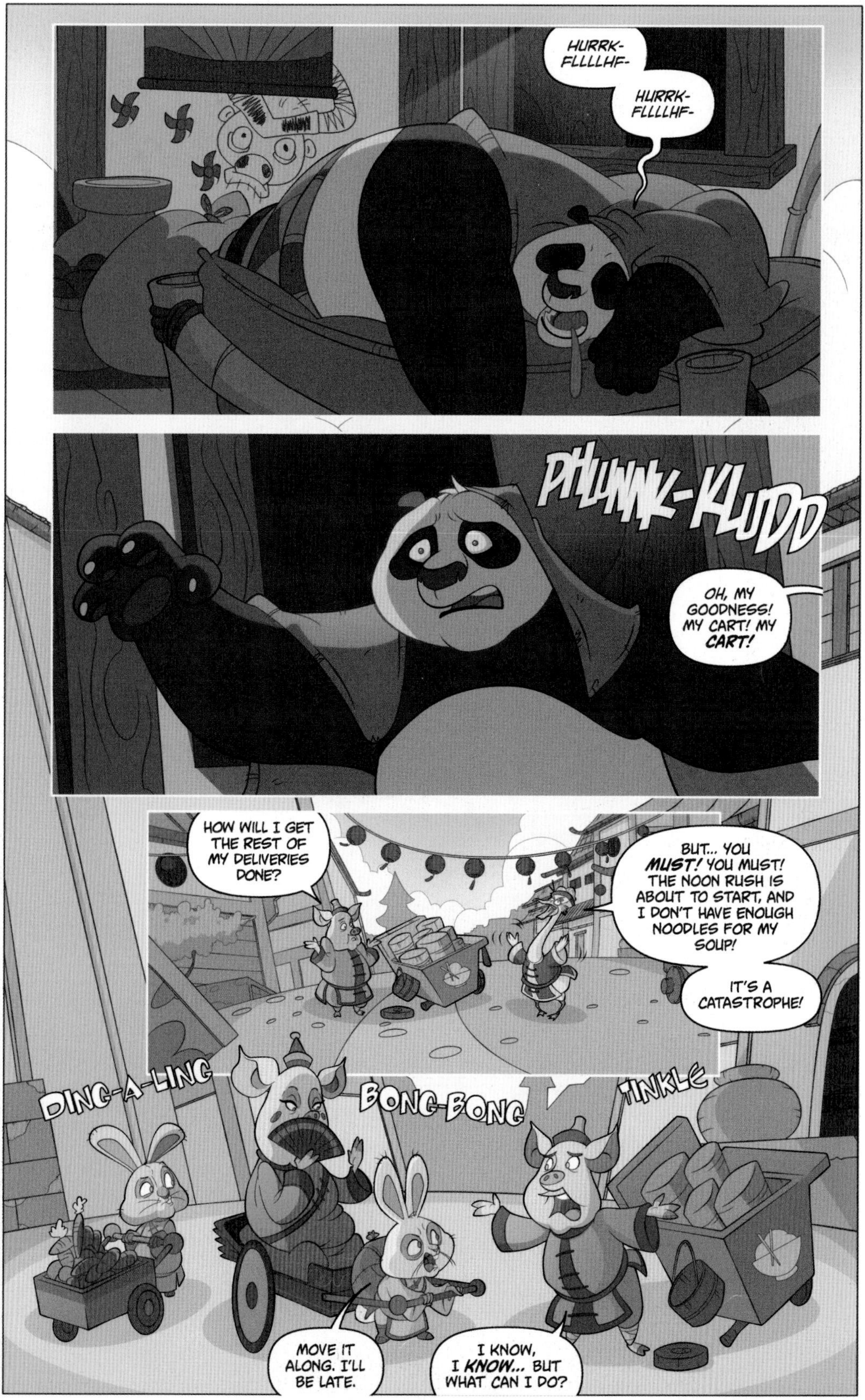
HURRK-
FLLLLHF-
HURRK-
FLLLLHF-
PHLUNNK-KLUDD
OH, MY GOODNESS! MY CART! MY *CART!*
HOW WILL I GET THE REST OF MY DELIVERIES DONE?
BUT... YOU *MUST!* YOU MUST! THE NOON RUSH IS ABOUT TO START, AND I DON'T HAVE ENOUGH NOODLES FOR MY SOUP!
IT'S A CATASTROPHE!
DING-A-LING
BONG-BONG
TINKLE
MOVE IT ALONG. I'LL BE LATE.
I KNOW, I *KNOW...* BUT WHAT CAN I DO?

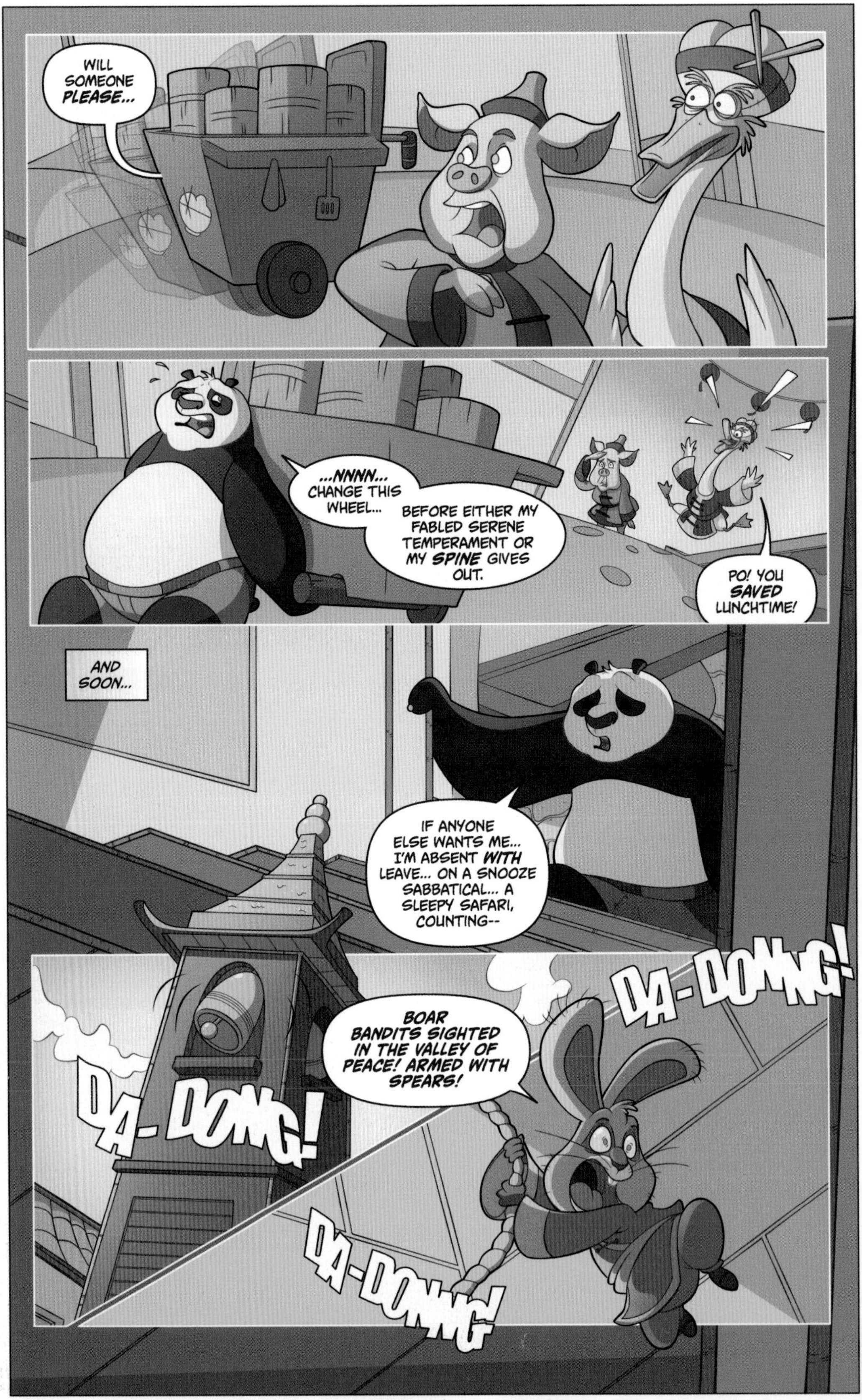
WILL SOMEONE PLEASE...
...NNNN... CHANGE THIS WHEEL...
BEFORE EITHER MY FABLED SERENE TEMPERAMENT OR MY SPINE GIVES OUT.
PO! YOU SAVED LUNCHTIME!
AND SOON...
IF ANYONE ELSE WANTS ME... I'M ABSENT WITH LEAVE... ON A SNOOZE SABBATICAL... A SLEEPY SAFARI, COUNTING--
DA-DONNG!
BOAR BANDITS SIGHTED IN THE VALLEY OF PEACE! ARMED WITH SPEARS!
DA-DONG!
DA-DONNG!

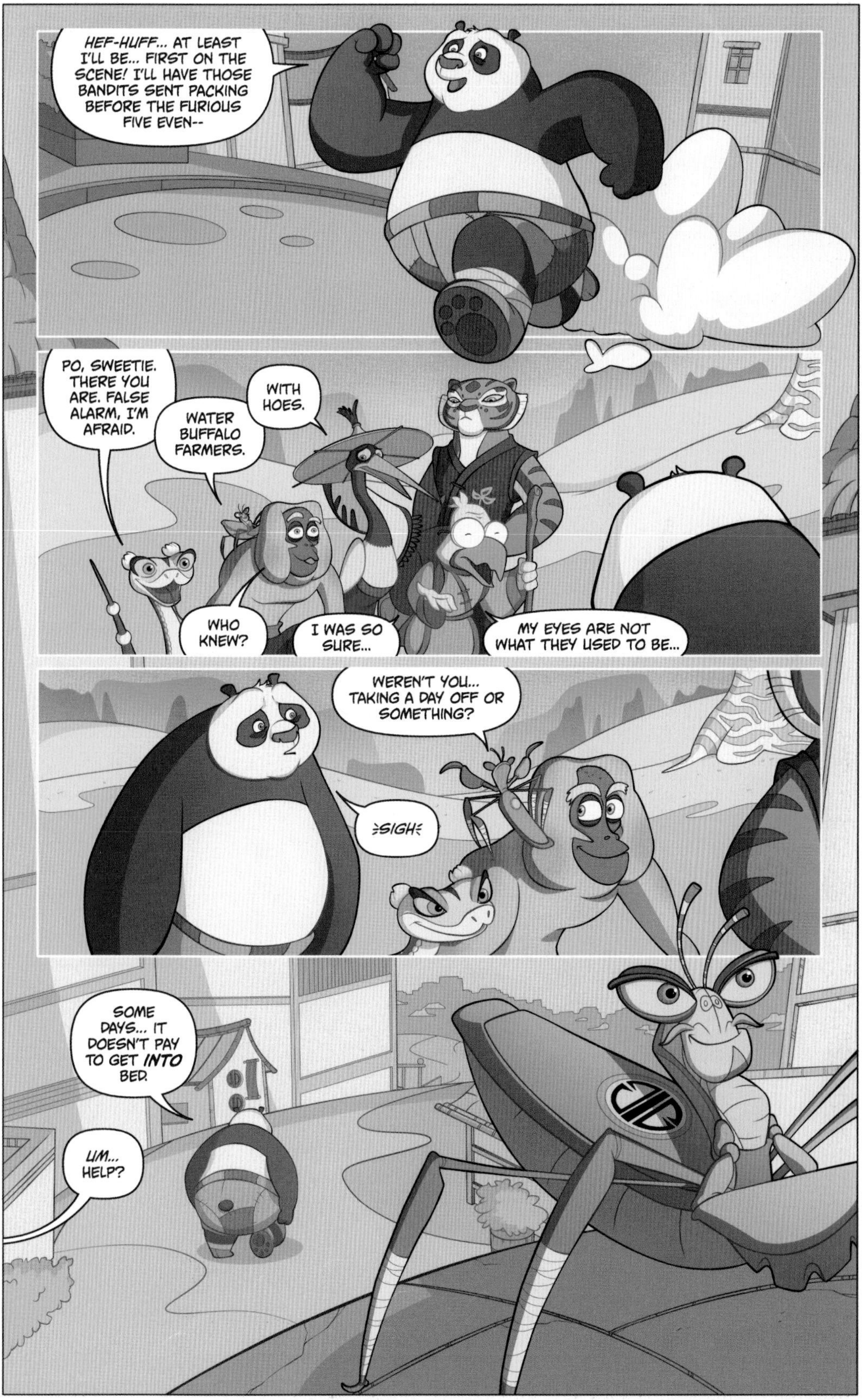
HEF-HUFF... AT LEAST I'LL BE... FIRST ON THE SCENE! I'LL HAVE THOSE BANDITS SENT PACKING BEFORE THE FURIOUS FIVE EVEN--
PO, SWEETIE. THERE YOU ARE. FALSE ALARM, I'M AFRAID.
WATER BUFFALO FARMERS.
WITH HOES.
WHO KNEW?
I WAS SO SURE...
MY EYES ARE NOT WHAT THEY USED TO BE...
WEREN'T YOU... TAKING A DAY OFF OR SOMETHING?
SIGH
SOME DAYS... IT DOESN'T PAY TO GET INTO BED.
UM... HELP?

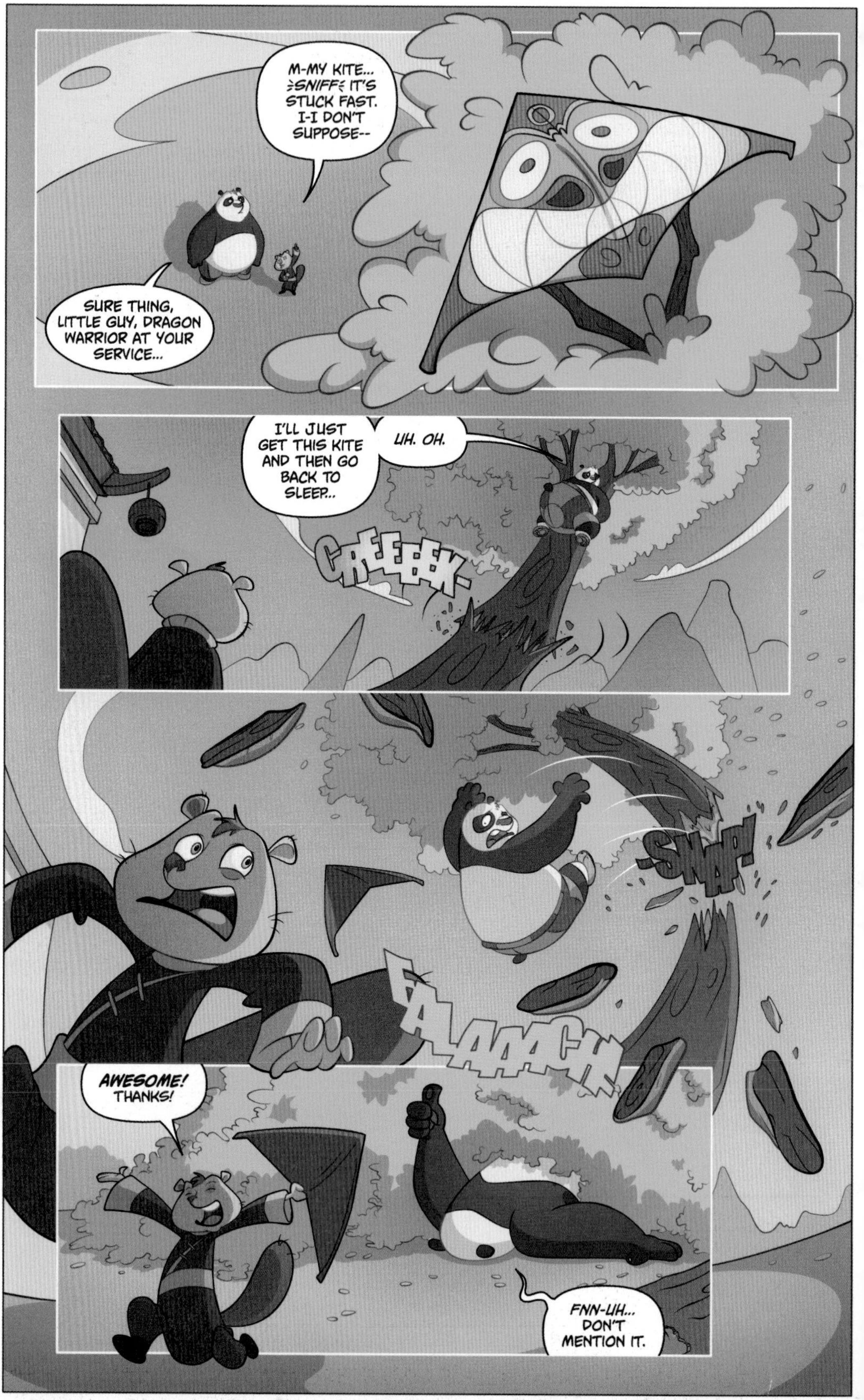
M-MY KITE... SNIFF IT'S STUCK FAST. I-I DON'T SUPPOSE--
SURE THING, LITTLE GUY, DRAGON WARRIOR AT YOUR SERVICE...
I'LL JUST GET THIS KITE AND THEN GO BACK TO SLEEP...
UH. OH.
CREEEEK-
-SNAP!
FAAAAACH
AWESOME! THANKS!
FNN-UH... DON'T MENTION IT.

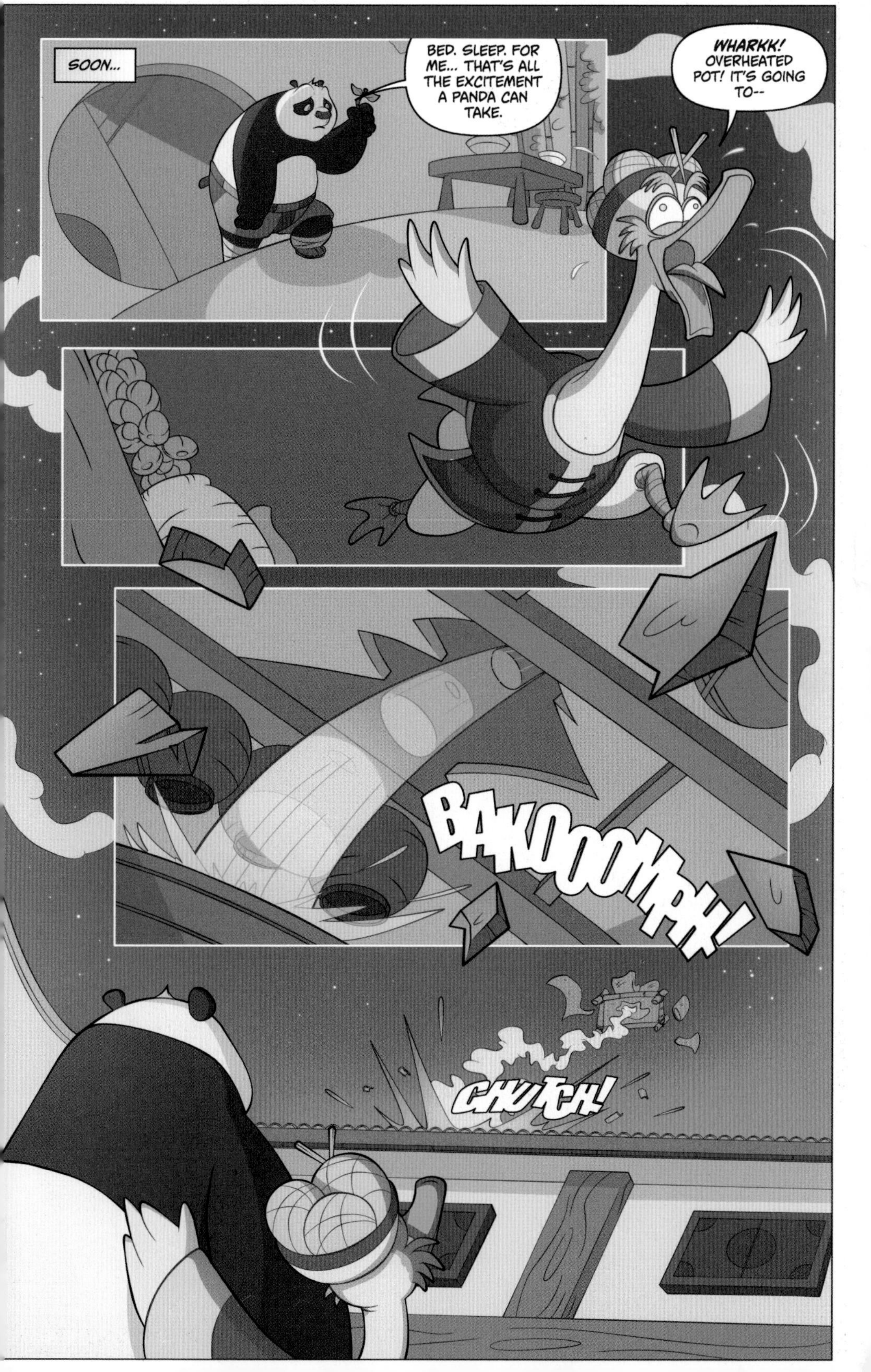
SOON...
BED. SLEEP. FOR ME... THAT'S ALL THE EXCITEMENT A PANDA CAN TAKE.
WHARKK! OVERHEATED POT! IT'S GOING TO--
BAKOOOOMPH!
CHUTCH!

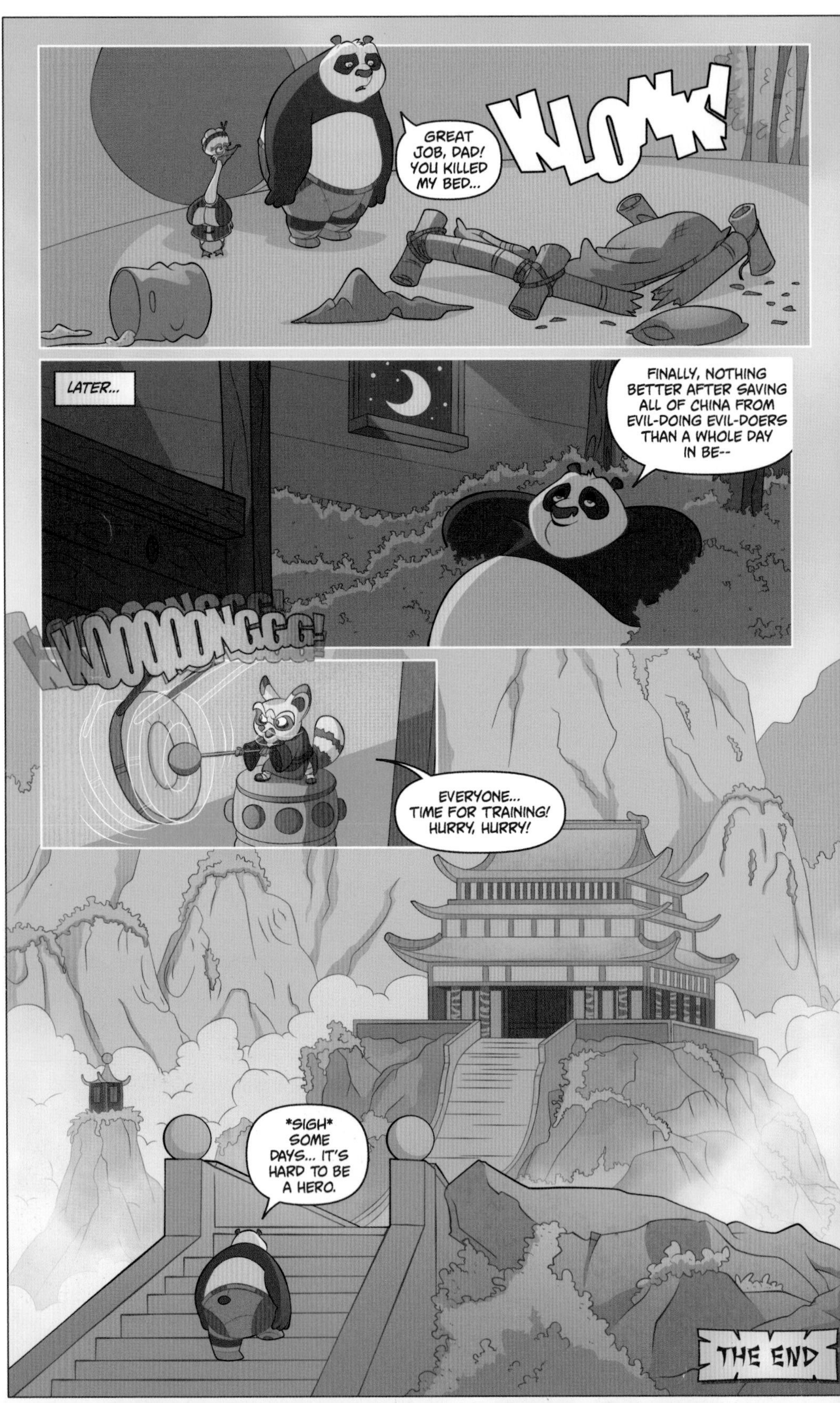
GREAT JOB, DAD! YOU KILLED MY BED...
KLONK!
LATER...
FINALLY, NOTHING BETTER AFTER SAVING ALL OF CHINA FROM EVIL-DOING EVIL-DOERS THAN A WHOLE DAY IN BE--
WHOOOOONGGG!
EVERYONE... TIME FOR TRAINING! HURRY, HURRY!
*SIGH* SOME DAYS... IT'S HARD TO BE A HERO.
THE END

# THE FURIOUS FIVE!

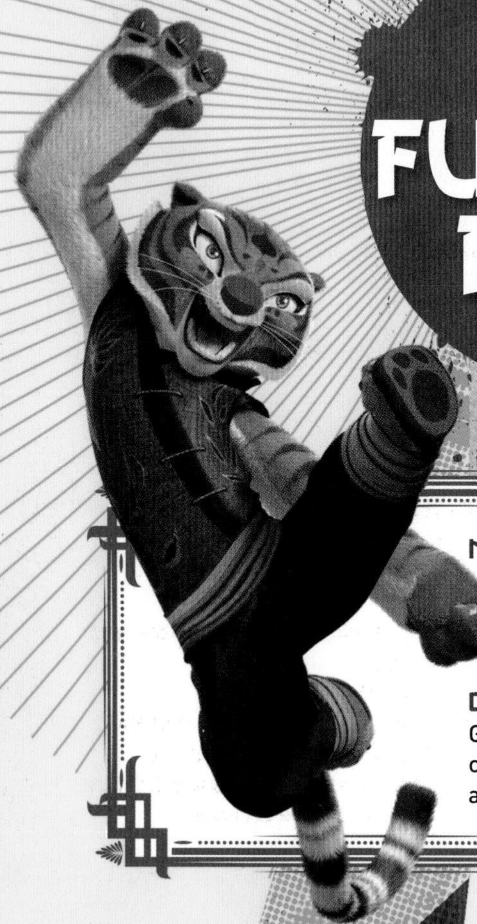

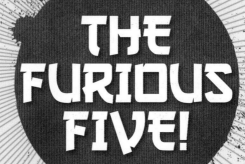

**NAME:** Master Tigress
**COMBAT STYLE:** Tiger Style
**FAMOUS MOVE:** Tahlia Leap (using a wall to run up and somersault off)
**FAVORITE FOOD:** Tofu stir-fry
**ORIGIN:** Master Shifu found her in the Bao Gu Orphanage. As a cub she had trouble controlling her temper, but he saw potential and decided to train her.

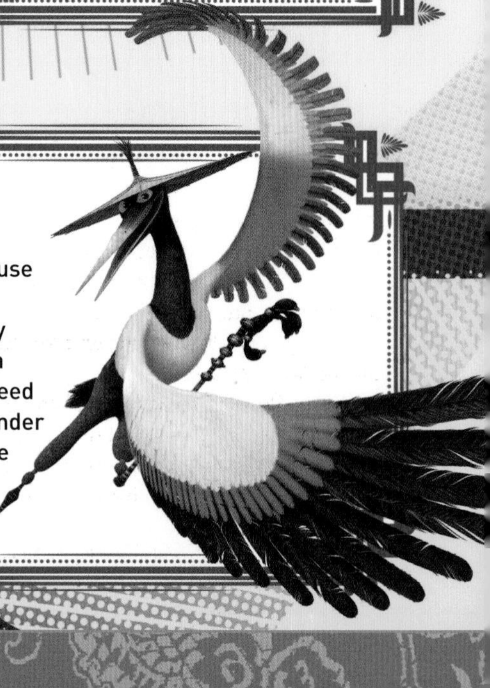

**NAME:** Master Crane
**COMBAT STYLE:** Crane Style
**SPECIAL SKILLS:** Ambidextrous – can use both talons for eating, writing etc.
**FAVORITE HOBBY:** Chinese calligraphy
**ORIGIN:** Originally a janitor at the Lee Da Kung Fu Academy, Crane worked with speed and accuracy, and discovered that his slender build enabled him to perform better in the rigorous obstacle course than the other Academy students.

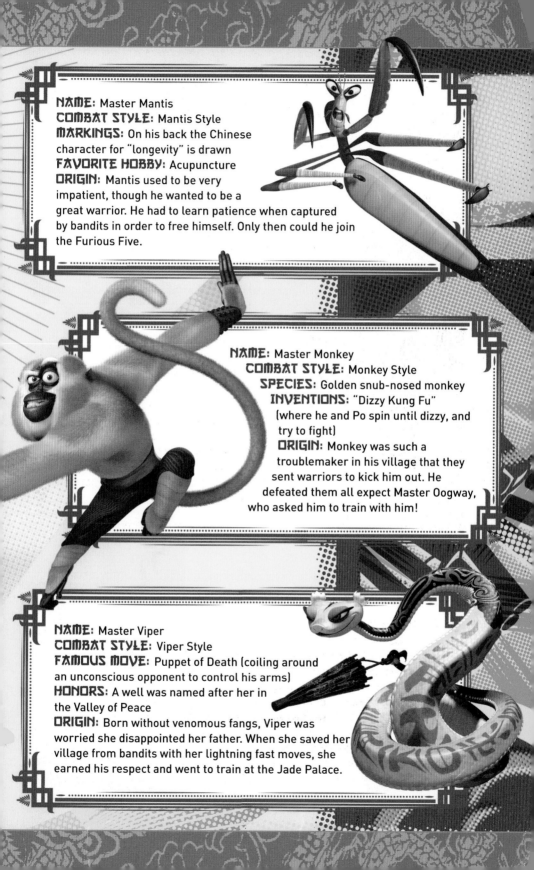

**NAME:** Master Mantis
**COMBAT STYLE:** Mantis Style
**MARKINGS:** On his back the Chinese character for "longevity" is drawn
**FAVORITE HOBBY:** Acupuncture
**ORIGIN:** Mantis used to be very impatient, though he wanted to be a great warrior. He had to learn patience when captured by bandits in order to free himself. Only then could he join the Furious Five.

**NAME:** Master Monkey
**COMBAT STYLE:** Monkey Style
**SPECIES:** Golden snub-nosed monkey
**INVENTIONS:** "Dizzy Kung Fu" (where he and Po spin until dizzy, and try to fight)
**ORIGIN:** Monkey was such a troublemaker in his village that they sent warriors to kick him out. He defeated them all expect Master Oogway, who asked him to train with him!

**NAME:** Master Viper
**COMBAT STYLE:** Viper Style
**FAMOUS MOVE:** Puppet of Death (coiling around an unconscious opponent to control his arms)
**HONORS:** A well was named after her in the Valley of Peace
**ORIGIN:** Born without venomous fangs, Viper was worried she disappointed her father. When she saved her village from bandits with her lightning fast moves, she earned his respect and went to train at the Jade Palace.

# MASTER SHIFU

**NAME:** Master Shifu

**SPECIES:** Red panda

**OCCUPATION:** Teacher and Master of the Jade Palace

**FAMILY:** Tai Lung (adopted son)

**KUNG FU MENTOR:** Formerly Master Oogway

**COMBAT STYLE:** Every style!

**FAMOUS MOVE:** Wuxi Finger Hold (overpowers an opponent just by holding their finger!)

**ABILITIES:** Super hearing (possibly due to large ears!)

## THE FURIOUS FIVE

The Valley of Peace has been protected by many different versions of the Furious Five for years. Shifu was once a member himself, and now he is the mentor of the current formation, consisting of Mantis, Crane, Viper, Monkey and Tigress.

## HIS ADOPTED SON

One day Master Shifu discovered an abandoned snow leopard outside the Jade Palace. He named him Tai Lung, and raised him as his own, training him in kung fu. He believed Tai Lung would become the Dragon Warrior, but Oogway disagreed. Tai Lung decided to try and take the title by force, ravaging the Valley of Peace, and devastating Shifu.

## THE DRAGON WARRIOR

When Po was selected as Dragon Warrior, Shifu was not convinced; "Oogway may have picked you, but when I'm through... you're going to wish he hadn't!" He put the panda through rigorous training to see if he'd quit, but Po proved determined, defeating Tai Lung in battle and saving Master Shifu's life.

# DREAMWORKS DIGESTS
# ALSO AVAILABLE

**Dreamworks Classics, Volume 1**

**Home Volume 1**

**Home Volume 2**

**Kung Fu Panda Volume 1**

**Kung Fu Panda Volume 2**

**Penguins of Madagascar, Vol 1**

**Penguins of Madagascar, Vol 2**

**DreamWorks Dragons: Riders of Berk, Vol 1**

**DreamWorks Dragons: Riders of Berk, Vol 2**

**DreamWorks Dragons: Riders of Berk, Vol 3**

**DreamWorks Dragons: Riders of Berk, Vol 4**

**DreamWorks Dragons: Riders of Berk, Vol 5**

3 1901 03696 0849

**DreamWorks Dragons: Riders of Berk, Vol 6**

**DreamWorks Dragons: Defenders of Berk Coming 22 March 2016**

# WWW.TITAN-COMICS.COM